THE INCUBUS & HIS HEART

MAFIA, MURDER, AND MAYHEM SERIES (AS A PREQUEL)

ELM JED

ELM JED

Cover Art by S.Wolf.Art

No AI was used in the writing, artwork, or creation of this novella.

Paperback ISBN - 9781967019212

Ebook ISBN - 9781967019205

Formatted with Vellum

To the readers who loved Pops and Ma more than the actual main characters

Contents

Book Playlist

"On the Nature of Daylight" - Max Richter
"Carry Me" - Eurielle
"Caribbean Blue" - Nomé Naku
"Davy Jones Theme- Intense Epic Version" -
Pianistec Cover, Hans Zimmer
"Fall for Me"- Sleep Token
"Zombie- Acoustic Version" - YUNGBLUD
"To the Gallows" - Secession Studios
"Gifts to Your Future Self" - Adam Dodson
"City on a Hill" - Mon Rovîa
"Promise" - HAEVN
"Blackheart" - Two Steps From Hell
"Love Me" - Yiruma
"Would You Fall in Love With Me Again (Epic Cinematic)-
Jay Putty, Matt Macleod & Kendra Dantes

Content Warnings

On page:
Slight blood and gore, death, burning buildings, slight PTSD flashbacks, harsh weather, and being attacked by Feral ghouls.

Discussed in this story:
Enslavement, abuse, death, & family disownment

Chapter One

"The path to paradise begins in Hell."
– Dante Alighieri

Alanzo watches as the home he built turns to ash.

Flames rise higher; branches snapping as they're consumed by the burning cottage. Anger pulses in his veins, threatening to release through his powers. It writhes in want to strike terror into those who'd done this. To bring them to their knees as their nightmares come alive within their minds. His hands threaten to flex and crush as smoke billows towards the heavens. The only reason he holds back, not returning to the monster he recently was, trembles in his arms with tears streaking her cheeks.

A year of attempting to rebuild a life together. Once more forced to start over.

Again.

Dawn approaches, the light of early day creeping through the mountain ranges and peaks. Alanzo's sharp violet eyes roam to the village in the distance, what *should* be their home, but exiled upon prejudice and disgust. The consequences of what he'd done followed him back to their original home. He had braced for it, far too used to the fear and displacement over the years. Except, their families had not been more horrified of what he'd done, but what *she'd* done. His Mate, this succubus who clings to him, who spent over five years a slave locked inside mines until he rescued her, was the forsaken one.

His arms tighten around Carmen, both in comfort and knowing. Alanzo knew she had used her powers to help ease other prisoners into death; stopping their suffering when pleaded. She and a handful of others had given that mercy in a place where none was given. All the while, she waited for him, whilst her family succumbed to despair without ever trying to find her. What she'd done was so egregious to them, that it didn't matter the horrors she witnessed. To the succubi and incubi of their home, she had done the worst possible action—assisted in giving death.

Alanzo reigns in his powers to keep them from lashing out once more.

He hoped over time that giving them a bit of distance between them and their families, relations would soften. They'd be welcome home again. Perhaps, over time they would learn to understand the choices both had made to survive. It was a small hope that they'd go back to their lives before being ripped apart. On the outskirts of the village, they remained quietly on their own over the past year, yearning to be welcome in those arms again.

No. Such a fate was not given to them.

The exile of their presence was loud in their family's silence.

They were met with sneers of disgust withered in hate. Doors shut in their faces. Food and goods removed from tables and wagons. And now, they've taken their home. Burned it to nothing; to begin once more with nothing.

Alanzo smooths his hand over her short dark hair, that which barely touches the nape of her neck. She keeps it short, or she becomes rife with fear of it being ripped from her head or being dragged across the ground. Her dark pink skin still appears too pale for him, even in the crackling firelight as shadows bounce off her short horns and smallish figure. His heart clenches for the one he loves beyond death.

He hates the sounds of her cries, reminding him too much of nights he wishes to forget.

No more.

They had tried and given their peace, receiving not even remnants of memories that they were once children of those across the field.

He cradles her face, lifting it for her to look upon him. Cobalt blue eyes, glassy with tears come to his.

"My heart, will you trust me?" He asks in a rough voice.

"Always," she whispers.

"We're leaving. Not a field away. A town. Or even a valley. We'll go beyond territories, through the mountains if we must. A place for us." Her eyes widen. "I will ask Giuseppe for supplies to travel this coming morning. We shall leave during the sunlight, while the others sleep."

She swallows hard, peering over her shoulder to the walls of the village. The place they both once called home years ago. The faint sunlight of dawn approaches as the flames crackle in the early light of day. The sky alights with pinks and oranges, a softer fire on the horizon than the one burning before them.

Barely, Alanzo can sense the change of her scent. The dampening that occurs when sadness comes with despair.

Carmen nods gently, burying her face into his chest. Alanzo holds her close, attempting to soothe her with his powers to ease her suffering. Except, he can't remember how. Months he's tried to reach that part of him, but it's vanished. Years of drowning himself in wrath, agony, and terror it was all he could ever conjure from the depths of his core. It came easily and effortlessly. Clutching his Mate, he felt broken away from that warmer side of himself, perhaps it never to be rekindled again.

Incubi and succubi were Paranormal beings created for two things— pleasure and pain. Most focused on the pleasure and desire of creatures, connected to those emotions which create bliss and joy. Their kind were revered in healing and comfort to their communities and towns filled with other Paranormal beings. While he'd taken the opposite path through pain. Alanzo didn't regret a single decision that led him to find Carmen, even if it meant he'd never tap into that piece of his powers again. Yet in these moments, he wished he could ease her pain beyond of holding and loving her. To take away her suffering, if just for a moment. Provide for her as so many incubi or succubi are able to give their Mates.

Monster. Murderer.

Inhaling sharply, Alanzo's wings shimmer into existence, flaring open behind him. The leathery wings create a dark shadow over them both as he glares into the crackling fire.

They will start over. They will be happy; without feeling hunted.

No more.

Chapter Two

"While there's life, there's hope."
– Marcus Tullius Cicero

Giuseppe had given them the bare essentials to travel a few weeks.

Alanzo's long-time friend, perhaps his only true ally in this part of the world, had held sadness on his face, but did not argue. He had nodded his head in understanding when Alanzo told him they were leaving.

The shifter with his pale green skin and tousled white hair had appeared disheveled when they arrived at his home. It was a few hours before high noon, perfect timing to prepare and then leave while there was enough light without navigating the evening sky from other flying Paranormal beings. The sky was clear, hopefully remaining as such while they would travel towards the mountains and away from this place.

Other an Giuseppe, there were no other friends or allies to them in the village. The gargoyles had left soon after Alanzo had all those years ago; the only beings apart from Giuseppe who would've given such kindness.

While the sun shone upon the earth, the rest of the Paranormals in the village were asleep in their homes. As Alanzo's and Carmen's cottage lay in ash.

A pack is secured to Alanzo's back as Carmen says goodbye to Giuseppe. Alanzo reigns in the territorial burning in his chest, watching her hug another. A minute passes longer than he can hold, and a low growl emanates from his throat. Giuseppe steps back easily from her, keeping a calm expression and not having an inkling of disgruntlement of his friend's reaction. The much older Paranormal comes over to Alanzo, shakes his hand and then embraces him without hesitation.

"To see you leave once more, feels wrong with our short time together since your return," Giuseppe says wearily.

"We shall never find peace here. We tried, my friend. *I* tried."

"I know. I know." He steps back from Alanzo, giving him a sympathetic smile. "You have centuries to live, you should not become a stone statue here."

"With the gargoyles gone, that would be harder to achieve," Alanzo says solemnly.

"Almost a jest, perhaps the old Alanzo is not fully gone." Their eyes meet, and Giuseppe's smile fades a little.

"Perhaps," Alanzo murmurs.

"May you find a place to call home and to finally be happy." Giuseppe smiles over to Carmen, serrated teeth glinting in the bright sunlight. "Both of you deserve as such."

"Thank you, Giuseppe," Carmen whispers.

"I will send word when we find what we are looking for," Alanzo says as Carmen steps over to him. "How I do not know, but I shall, my friend."

Giuseppe hums, then asks, "Will you travel once more across the seas or further north towards Wallachia? I hear the vampires and gargoyles are not too troublesome there."

Alanzo's face darkens, briefly remembering his times through the Polish Kingdoms. Troublesome the Paranormals may not be, but there was too much war in that direction. It was why the gargoyle families here had left. They'd flown to fight in battles against humans and Paranormals alike. Many were squabbling over territories, especially the humans. In the last decade, it felt that too many kingdoms were falling. The world was changing quickly.

"No," Alanzo finally answers. "Not that far north."

"Then you'll remain in Italy?"

Alanzo takes Carmen's hand, and she gives him a soft look. His expression becomes earnest as he answers for them, "Yes. We shall stay in our home country. Our families have exiled us, but not our homeland."

Giuseppe sighs. "Stay away from the southern borders and seas. There is worry of the Ottomans coming to these shores. Humans will fight their wars, but it does not promise they shall not force us into their battles. A truth you must know."

"I do. Far too much," Alanzo sighs. "Thank you, my friend."

"May your journey be safe and true."

With their final goodbyes, Alanzo picks up Carmen into his arms. Her own wrap around his neck and shoulders, pressing herself into his thick tunic. They're both dressed warmly for the high altitude and harsh winds that will come with flying. Alanzo's wings with a powerful thrust, lift them into the air. They soar into the sky as the village they had grown up within becomes smaller and smaller, until he turns away and flies north towards the mountains.

Carmen's body tightens, pressing against Alanzo as he glides through the clouds. He gives a final look to what should have been home, but only sees the ash and burnt wood of the house he built with his own hands. Anger pulses through him, surging him forward to find a home they could be happy and safe.

Too many years they had endured.

Too many years of being separated and without each other's strength.

In his heart, Alanzo knew they were destined to have their peace. If only he knew exactly where such a place would be.

Chapter Three

"Passion is the genesis of genius."
– Galileo Galilei

For hours he flies as the sun shines through the clouds. Alanzo's skin warms from the direct sunlight. He's always favored the daylight over the night. One of the other reasons why so many Paranormals, not just the incubi and succubi, have remained at a distance from him years past. Long before he'd become a monster that hunted across the world, he had been an outcast. A term he had grown used to, but not his Carmen.

Before the true monsters came in the night, stealing her and others from their homes, she *belonged* in the village. She had been a succubus who was respected and beloved. A being that many had fawned and fallen over. When she had agreed to be his Mate, while both were so early in age, it had caused an uproar. Her family and even his were known for their multiple partners and lovers, as many do of incubi and succubi, but not them. Alanzo could not fathom loving anyone other than her. He knew the moment he laid eyes upon her, there would be no other for his soul to cherish. There was no one else he wanted to spend the rest of his lifetime with; centuries to live or not.

Wind shifting and picking up in speed, Alanzo flicks his gaze to the west. Storm clouds build, growing darker as a flash of lightning splits the grey in the distance. He swerves away from the west, aiming downward to the tree lines that come into view along the low hills.

"Alanzo?"

"We must find shelter for the night. Rain is coming. Hold on, my heart." Her grip intensifies as he flies closer to the forests.

His eyes search for anything to hide within. Finally, he notices towering rock that could give prospect to a cave system below. Shifting within the air, he turns and flies towards where the clouds gather above the hills. Maneuvering easily, Alanzo guides them through the trees until he lands upon delicate feet before the high wall of hard earth. Glancing towards the forming darkness of clouds above, his sight moves down the wall of rock and comes upon a cave entrance not far from them. He walks towards it, powers pulsing out of him like shadows which stretch over the distance that searches for emotions to subdue animals or other threats.

Carmen adjusts in his arms, and then teases gently, "I can walk, my knight."

"I'd rather carry you."

"Your arms must be tired. Allow me to walk."

"I shall carry you even when my arms do not move anymore or if they are torn from my body. I'll never tire having you in my arms, my heart." A ghost of a smile drifts over his face, and she returns the expression just as faintly.

Alanzo's powers flicker over the cave entrance, and a moment he pauses just outside of it. Again, he searches through the hovering of his powers for signs of life and finds no hint of it within. Empty. He dips down into the smaller entrance of the cave, finally setting Carmen upon her feet once he sees the back wall of dark hardened stone. His pack is pulled off next, while the rumble of thunder comes from outside in the distance. The smell of rain follows next, mixing with the scent of dirt and hardened clay. The cave itself is dim, soon to be engulfed in darkness unless he finds a source to create light.

"Stay here. I will gather wood," he instructs.

Carmen gives a simple nod as he pulls out the only weapon he has—a sword forged specially for him. The handle is carved out of silver and another metal he does not know the name of, as he was never told. It fit within his hand perfectly, crafted precisely for his palm. The shifter who created it would not tell him much of how it was forged, speaking only that it was a secret for shifters alone. For now. What Alanzo did know was that the metal of the blade could cleave through a gargoyle's stone hide.

Two words were etched into the length of the blade on either side: cuore and bella.

Names he had for Carmen years ago. They then became the reminders of who he searched for through the years. A decision not made by him, but by the shifter out of hope that Alanzo would not lose himself completely to the monster he'd become. A villain that would be scorned and hunted for the deeds he would commit. A hope to not fall into a darkness that would have him destroy armadas and towns in search of his Mate.

The shifter was perhaps correct in doing so. For many moments, Alanzo would look upon the etched in words and find the purpose that drove him when his strength waned.

Alanzo pauses at the cave entrance, glancing down at the glinting silver within the fading light. Inhaling deep, he shoves away the horrific memories that try to gather, and then leaves to find wood. He doesn't go far, not daring to leave too much space between him and Carmen. Finding her would not be the issue, it is the panic that surges up his spine. The nightmarish horrors of isolation and dread that had filled his core for years attempt to return when a sliver of isolation appears.

He does not take long gathering wood and returns to the cave right before the pouring of rain reaches them. Wind and rain rage outside as the fire is lit, casting shadows over the deep earthen walls with speckles and lines of grey stone. Carmen sets together a quick meal of dried meat and bread as darkness falls. Wind whistles outside through the trees, making the leaves rattle.

It's far later when Alanzo stands sentry near the entrance, watching the storm outside. Carmen sits upon a blanket laid out, placing another piece of wood into the fire. It crackles, embers floating up.

"Come lay down," she murmurs. "You have barely rested since we started."

"I have rested more these past few months than I have in years." He gives her a soft look. "You sleep."

"You can sleep in my arms..." she swallows, pulling the other blanket they have over her legs, "...for I cannot carry you, my knight."

Alanzo's expression gentles more as he looks upon her. Firelight shines in her cobalt eyes, misting a little as he sees the guilt within them. He senses it there first before feeling her emotions in the air like a misting of rain you don't expect.

He breathes deep, glancing out of the cave. Once more his powers reach out, searching for any danger or cause for worry. Nothing. It is quiet with the heavy rain that falls, certainly making other creatures hide within their hovels much as they are in the cave. Relenting his position of sentry, he steps away and comes to sit beside her. His arm goes around his Mate as he leans back against the rigid rock wall.

It is quiet between them apart from the storm and small popping bursts of cinders. Carmen leans into his side, laying her head upon his shoulder.

"Do you know what you are searching for?" Her voice is tender, staring at the crackling fire. "Or where we are going?"

"Our home."

"And where is our home, my knight?"

Alanzo hums to himself, eyes glimpsing towards the blazing light. Deep embers of orange peek out through the charred wood at the bottom.

"A valley," he answers. "Somewhere that is tucked away from the world. A place where there's a stream or brook for us to bathe in. Wash our clothes and vegetables. A place for you to plant your garden to grow whatever your heart desires. And of course...for you to have flowers."

"Flowers?"

"Yes. For you love them, my life." He strokes back her short hair, careful in how he touches the nape of her neck. Her skin shivers, but she does not move. "Or it could have a meadow, where wildflowers will grow upon their own for you."

Carmen looks at him, noticing the sharpness of his cheekbones as the firelight creates shadows across his face. Although he is still quite young as an incubus, Alanzo appears far older than he is. His onyx hair is tousled from flying most of the day, and now slightly wet from standing guard near the entrance. His maroon skin is darker in the shadows of the cave, which within the dimness his violet eyes glow brilliantly. There are laugh lines from long ago, but he rarely smiles of late. From time to time, she has seen the expression, but only in small instances and always brief and small.

As if he has forgotten how.

The faint smiles he does have are for Carmen alone. Now, there are frown lines and crinkles of crow's feet near the edges of his eyes. One could easily assume he was a hundred years older than he was.

Neither of them have even reached to witness thirty years yet.

Carmen's heart sinks. Once more, as many times in the past year, recognizing that the Alanzo she knew was gone. He was still Alanzo in a sense, but she wondered if she would ever again see the smiling, carefree incubus she had initially fallen in love with.

Her face begins to fall, turning away to stare at the dancing flames.

"What is it, my love?" he asks gently.

The wind blows, whistling through trees as branches creak. A twig snaps, falling off and tumbling past the entrance. She shudders a moment, tensing as he holds her closer against his warm body.

"Do you believe Giuseppe?"

"Believe him in what?"

"That we will live for centuries?" She asks tentatively.

"I do. Do you not?"

She swallows hard, fear creeping over her skin. Alanzo does his best not to gravitate towards the emotions he senses; the ache emanating from her. Her emotions swirl briefly, bringing a scent of soured blossoms. No, not soured. Flowers drenched in the rain, close to the edge of drowning or rotting away.

Carmen does not pull her gaze away from the fire. Her mind slowly remembering of what was not long enough ago.

"Almost six years does not...it should not feel this heavy," she answers in a rasped tone. "Yet, that time stolen from us, weighs more than my entire childhood. Pieces of me taken that I cannot grasp anymore. Pieces of you. Will those years become lighter in a century's time? Or will it sharpen the hole those years created... hollowing it out further?"

Alanzo's breath catches, his eyes now upon the burning wood. His voice is rough, answering, "I do not know."

Silence returns.

The fire burns, wood breaking down as the light fades a little within the small space.

It is Alanzo who breaks the quiet between them.

"Hollow or filled, we shall endure together. We will replace the loss of those pieces with new. With growth. With life."

"And what if you tire of me?"

"Tire of you?"

"Neither of us are fools. For we both know that no incubus... has ever stayed forever with one being."

"Then I shall be the first." Alanzo tips her head back, meeting her gentle gaze. "I shall never tire of you, whether we live another ten years or a thousand. For didn't I promise you a thousand years, my heart?"

Tears form in her eyes. She blinks, and a singular tear falls down her cheek, catching the firelight before Alanzo wipes it away with his thumb.

"Yes, you did," she whispers.

"Will you tire of me?"

"No, because you promised me a thousand years."

Carmen reaches up, placing her hand against his upon her cheek. She closes her eyes, breathing in deeply the damp, earthen air.

"I hate that we had to leave our home, and our families," she says in a broken whisper. Alanzo's face falls, eyes dimming in the light. "I do not and shall never hate you, my knight. For you are the only being whom I believe shall keep his word. You, I believe, would keep a foolish thousand-year promise."

"Foolish, perhaps. But only to those who think it is." Alanzo brings his head forward, touching his with hers. Both their eyes are shut, inhaling each other's faint scents.

"I will build you a home, Carmen," Alanzo vows quietly. "Where no one may burn it to ash. I promise."

Chapter Four

"Rule your mind or it will rule you."
- Horace

Dawn's light is muted by the storm's clouds. The rain has fallen harder, pounding against the ground and seeping into the dirt. In the middle of the night, Alanzo moved their little fire further back into the cave as he could. Puddles filled the entryway, creating a natural moat that was becoming several feet wide. Worry fills Alanzo as he glances at the wood he was able to gather the night before. It could last another night, but if the rain continues into the next morning, they'd be left without a fire and source of warmth. It was spring, but the nights brought a chill, and the rain dropped the temperatures further.

Carmen sleeps upon his lap, curled beneath the blanket. He leans his head against the rock, closing his eyes in hopes of more sleep. They'll be stuck here until the rain passes, unable to fly with how strong the winds roar through the forest outside.

Memories begin to run across his mind. Nights and days where the rain had fallen like this. Moments in taverns, sailing through treacherous waters, hiding under his cloak in forests and rough terrain, or even flying through the dangerous clouds. Those years meld together as a long nightmare that seemed to never end. It was all consuming. The desperation mixed with fury as he searched for Carmen through new lands and waters. The world he had once known was no longer small, but far more vast with its mountains, seas, deserts, and forests.

And then there was the blood.

The screams and death that followed in his wake.

Haunted shadows of his deeds have become forever stitched upon his skin until his final breath. No matter how long he lived, decades or centuries, it would never leave him. Final breath after final breath where his hands rarely ever wielded his blade, yet he took so much life. It was his unchecked power of terror and anguish that stole lives. Alanzo had become a horror in the minds of man and Paranormal beings, to the point they'd plunge to their deaths in the water, slash their own throats, or through other unnatural ways to escape the terror he curated inside them. A living nightmare.

Kraken of the Red Sea.

Alanzo was *the* monster in the night. He was the legend and warning sailors gave to others sailing through the seas and oceans. The one they kept watch for. The one they whispered of in taverns and ports.

Almost six years, he was known only as the Kraken. His actual name a forgotten plea on his lips. He refused to take it back until he found her. Until he could hear it from her tongue again.

His eyes snap open when there's a flash of lightning. Inhaling deep, he listens to the crack of thunder that echoes through the other sounds of the storm. Carmen curls further in herself, clutching at Alanzo's side as he gently smooths his hand over her shoulders. She trembles a moment as he strokes her hair next.

"Calm, my love. You are safe," he whispers, running his hand over her head once more. Her body relaxes, easing against him.

The ache he used to feel dissipates as he watches her sleep. For all the bodies and sea of blood that trailed after him, he felt no remorse or guilt. He had felt nothing for years when they died, including the now. All that had mattered was her.

If fate was cruel enough to take her again...he would scorch the earth beyond saving.

Another crack of thunder rumbles through the forest. The sound is followed by the crackling of the fire, dimming a bit from the lack of fresh wood. He should put another piece in, but he does not want to disturb her.

His hand tenderly strokes over her arm.

"The cottage will be small." Alanzo begins to speak to himself quietly, easing further back against the dirt as he continues to caress her gently. "A corner within for us to sleep. A place to eat. A place to cook and bake. There'll be two sheds. One to prepare food for the colder months, and another to hold all the firewood and seedlings. I'll build a window of where we'll cook, so I may always see you when you bake your bread or when you garden. I shall find seeds to plant trees for fruits. Pears, strawberry, hmmm...perhaps figs. We will grow grapes with our own small vineyard, perhaps the hill will be on the side of the cottage. Of course, we will grow our crops away a little from us, but your garden will be closer. A forge will keep our home warm on brisk nights, and it shall smell heavenly with your baking."

"And what will I bake, my knight?" Carmen's soft voice drifts across the space.

Alanzo hums, not stopping in his caress over her shoulders.

"Your favorites because I will grow you the best wheat and grain. When you are feeling divine, then any of your wonderful pies and tarts."

"From the fruit trees you'll plant for me?"

"Yes, my heart."

"You'll eat them all?" She muses a little.

"Until you can roll me down the hill."

She sighs in amusement. "There will be a hill?"

"Yes, because we shall have our own vineyard."

A chuckle almost leaves her, but not quite. Carmen does not move from her spot laying upon Alanzo, watching as the rain picks up yet again. The moat at the entrance appears to grow slightly, splashing from the falling rain and water streaming down the rock side.

Worry flits over Alanzo again of the cave flooding if the rain does not relent.

"This cave reminds me of years ago." Carmen's voice pulls Alanzo's worried thoughts to her instead. His eyes do not leave the rippling water.

"How so?" He asks.

"Do you not remember?" There is trepidation in her voice.

Alanzo pulls his gaze down to her, forgetting the rising water as he finds her tender gaze. The blue of gemstones softly watch him, almost glowing even with the lack of light within the small space and storm outside.

His chest squeezes, realizing what she speaks of and feels an emotion he has not felt in quite a long time.

A good, pleasant memory.

A wonderful one that had been locked away out of pain and torment, from fear that such a moment would never occur again with her. Even now as his mind tries to hold a candle to the almost forgotten images and emotions, he feels unsure if it is something they'll ever share again.

The first time they'd lain together. The first time his hands had touched her as her own explored the dips and curves of his muscles. He had known nothing, never have letting another be with him. But she had, for Carmen like many within their village were traditional incubi and succubi, whilst he was not. He remembers the trickling feeling of relief that she knew what to do, and what to expect. He would've been lost without her, and a bumbling novice.

"I remember. My love, my life."

A gentleness comes over her, features softening once more and the trepidation vanishing.

The cave they once were in was not due to a storm like this, but to hide from their families after spending a day foraging flowers. The voices of their families had drifted in the distance, almost unrecognizable in Alanzo's memories as they ran to their hideaway. In the dawn's brilliant light of morning, they decided to be forever tied.

The distant memory feels like a faded fabric from being under the sun too long. Yet, he could recall the shiver of his skin. His lips against hers and anywhere else he could place them upon her. He truly did not know what he was doing, new to such intimacy, but she helped him well.

Alanzo hadn't meant to wait back then, unlike others of his kind. He had not wanted that intimacy with anyone else, until her. Carmen was all he ever wanted and felt this yearning in his soul that this succubus he would love only. Their love had been beautiful. And their first time laying together it was...awkward. Painful from him falling back onto some rocks. Most of all joyous.

Yes, Alanzo could remember it, even with how well locked it away those memories have been.

Carmen reaches up, touching his chin as she trails her fingers down his throat. The touch is soothing as the rain falls outside. Tenderly, he takes her hand and holds it against his chest.

Neither of them are ready for that intimacy again.

Far too much pain lingered in their bones and souls, shadows that followed too closely. For now, they will lean into the quiet of companionship and love. Until, hopefully, one day they would both be ready. And it would not be within *this* cave.

A loud crack of thunder echoes, followed by three more that shake the trees outside. Each rumbling sound closer than the last, almost shaking the ground next. Carmen's face whips to the entrance, eyes wide at the growing water that stretches for their fire.

"Let us hope it ends soon," Alanzo murmurs, wind picking up outside. "Or we may become a little wet ourselves, my heart."

Chapter Five

"Men are driven by two principal impulses, either by love or fear."
– Niccolò Machiavelli

There's screaming.

The smell of water, churning and splashing against the side of the boat. A deep chill engulfs Alanzo as the ship jolts into the water. Another bang and crash as barrels fall from below deck. The screams come again.

Again.

Blood seeping into the wood, flowing as heavily as the sea that splashes upon the ship—

"Alanzo!"

His true name jolts him out of his slumber, waking to feel the touch of water at his feet. Carmen grips him as he quickly stands, tension coiling through his shoulder and down into his stomach. The cave is dark, fire long gone as it's been drowned by the puddle that has turned into a lake within the cave. The edge of the water has come closer to them. In the darkness, he shifts his vision to better look at the rising water.

"Gather the supplies," he says calmly, looking towards the darkness outside. It's late within the night, but the rain has lessened to a misting drizzle.

"Where will we go?"

"Hopefully a place where we shall not have to swim." Alanzo helps pack their bag, pulling it onto his shoulders and then securing his sword. Swiftly, he picks Carmen up, who gasps under her breath.

"Hold onto me, my heart." Her arms tighten around his neck as he steps into the small pond. The water is not deep, but it does reach past his knees as he gets closer to the entrance. The bone chilling water seeps into him, threatening to make him shiver as he makes his way to the entrance. It splashes around his legs as he ventures out of the cave and into the drizzling rain. The water that has accumulated keeps stretching further into the forest as he glances up at the night sky, attempting to determine what time it is as droplets fall upon his face. Unable to see any stars or even the moon, he continues forward.

"Can you fly in this?" She asks as he strides through the chilly water that surrounds them.

"No. It is too cold to fly. The clouds and rain may gather ice upon my wings."

Carmen shivers as she grips onto him. Alanzo navigates towards the edge of the water, finally coming to the end of the flooding. He steps out of the forming lake that has grown in the past two days of rain. His legs are freezing but he ignores the chill as he continues and gives them a good distance from the risen water. Once he comes under a tree, he sets Carmen upon her feet.

Light rain mists over them, dripping through the branches to wet their faces and hair further. Alanzo's hands are careful as he grabs the hood of her cloak, pulling it up over her head. Blue eyes within the shadows of the hood gaze up at him, filled with fear. His face remains calm as he tucks back strands of her hair, adjusting her hood to protect her face more from the rain.

He was damp, soaked from his thighs down and bitterly cold, but he had endured worse than this. He hides the shivers his body wants to create, ignoring it as he takes her hand.

"We will keep walking until dawn," he says. "With luck, the storm may fully break, and we'll be drier when daylight comes. Do not worry, my love, we shall not be wet for long."

Her faint smile can be seen even in the darkness.

Alanzo guides them through the trees in hopes of less rain falling upon them. Their steps are quiet as they venture through the forest. Leaves rustle in the wind, while branches creak far above them as they scrape against the other. Light pattering of rain surrounds them in the night as they travel through the unfamiliar woods.

Constantly, Alanzo's powers stretch out around them, searching for threats. The invisible shadows are met with only the life of trees, shrubbery, and hiding animals. Silence looms through the forest as they travel through the final hours of the storm. Branches snap from time to time as the trees rustle with every stiff breeze. Every pierce into the quiet, Carmen grips her hand tighter around Alanzo's fingers. Her body brushes against his, trembling a bit in fear. Each time she does, he reassures her gently.

The rain turns into a mist as they approach a small meadow within the woods. Beyond the tree line, Alanzo can see the faint glow of morning coming. The light blue haze has a pale orange on the very edge of the horizon, struggling to be seen through the last of the clouds. He stops them at the edge of the meadow beneath a large tree, glimpsing up into the cloudy sky.

"We'll wait here until more light comes. The meadow is perfect to ascend from."

Carmen steps further under the tree's shadow, bending down to feel the ground upon the hopes of discovering a dry spot. She finds one right against the trunk of the tree, but then there's a howl in the distance. Another follows, far closer than the first.

Both become still.

"Behind me, my heart." Alanzo's voice is rough as she stands fully, moving in place behind him as he maneuvers for the tree to be at her back.

Alanzo pulls in his powers, keeping them close as he waits for the predators lurking in the morning haze. Carefully, he pulls out his sword next. The light weapon is steady in his hands as he holds it at his side, blade almost dull in the mist. There's a growl straight ahead, and then another following suit from farther left of the meadow. Narrowing his eyes, Alanzo searches the tree line of the meadow, finding no movement. He can feel the creatures though, cautiously touching upon their emotions of hunger and survival.

Wolves.

His powers flit over another, searching for the familiar signs of the intelligence of a Paranormal being. Not werewolves or shifters. Just wolves.

The scent of Alanzo's powers surround them as he straightens, filling the air with a thick smokey smell that's tinged in metal. Carmen presses against his back as he moves his arm behind him, caressing her arm in reassurance.

These animals were nothing in comparison of what he has stood against, but even he knew packs of any kind should not be trifled with. The wolves were close to having them surrounded, including about to block their way out of the woods.

Alanzo's eyes begin to glow as the wolves' growls fill the meadow and once quiet forest, making the rest of the noise vanish. One of them finally steps into the meadow, and then another. Another. Two more. An entire pack reveals themselves as a few bare their teeth at the Paranormals upon the other edge. Two wolves start to stalk forward, licking their lips. Suddenly, they freeze with a quick whine.

The scent of burning metal and smoke fills the air, spreading past Alanzo and Carmen into the rest of the meadow. It's the only warning from Alanzo's powers before fear twists into the wolves' minds. A foreign emotion to them perhaps, but instincts can kick in when one knows they have become the prey. Confusion is the next feeling thrusted upon them, causing one to yelp and then quickly turns to bite another wolf. They start to fight each other, while a couple whimper and whine as they shove themselves into the ground. Their growls change into the sound of teeth tearing into fur and barking as Alanzo glares at the threat.

Kill them. Protect her. An old voice in Alanzo's mind trickles through his ears.

"Alanzo." Carmen's whisper is soft, not quite a plea.

The wolves keep fighting. Terror and confusion emboldened inside them as Alanzo's powers strengthen, latching onto the strong, instinctual emotions. Burning metal fills the air, replacing the smell of fallen rain and damp earth.

Destroy them. The voice in Alanzo's head becomes more emboldened.

"Alanzo." Her grip tightens upon his arm as she watches with wide eyes. Her Mate does not move as his powers make the wolves fight each other, spilling blood upon the grass. The creatures tear at each others throats and legs, whimpering and yelping through pain.

The incubus does not halt their fighting. He does not move as he easily manipulates what was once a threat, now becoming his prey. In the far reaches of his mind, those growls and whimpers merge with screams and crying. Familiar. Those sounds are far too familiar. Blood stained comfort. A toxic balm to the far reaches of his mind. He feels himself falling into the abyss he once drowned in, allowing the growing sense of power that came with the control of—

"Alanzo. Stop."

He blinks.

The glow of Alanzo's eyes ease as he glimpses over his shoulder at his Mate. The territorial need to protect her weighing heavy in his chest, but it clenches in sorrow when he sees her gaze. Realization comes that it was not protective instinct driving him to destroy the wolves, but the terror starving monster he had once was when she was lost.

"Don't kill them," she whispers gently.

"They would've—"

"Let them go, my love."

Unable to go against her wishes, Alanzo faces the wolves and shifts his powers. The grip he has on them releases, and a cacophony of whimpers fills the woods. Swiftly, all the wolves turn and bolt out of the meadow. They run, escaping the incubus that so few have been able to say they have. Quiet fills the woods once more as the light mist falls and the faint light of dawn approaching closer.

Alanzo completely reigns in his powers, pulling them deep

within himself as he feels his eyes dim from their glow. He averts his eyes from her, scowling at the ground. His jaw muscles tighten as the clenching in his chest does not relent. For the first time, in quite a long time, he feels finally feels that remorse. Guilt begins to seep into him for almost killing the wolves, more to add to the list of those destroyed by his powers. And then, the feeling of fear comes next.

Not of those wolves. Not of himself or once more becoming that monster he created again. The horror of scaring her. Of making her fear him. He could live with the sea of blood behind him, but not the potential terror of his beloved Mate.

"There's enough light to fly," he speaks in a rough voice. "The sun should warm the air, and we shall not worry over ice."

He starts to walk towards the middle of the meadow, putting his sword away at his side.

"Alanzo." Carmen reaches for his arm, stopping him from taking more than a few steps.

He does not flinch or move away, rooted in that very spot as she reaches up to touch his cheek. Gently, her fingers caress his tense jaw, having him look at her. No emotion flicks over his face. It is as though he was carved from stone; a mask of nothing. He begins to open his mouth to speak, but no words leave him.

What was there to say? Silence is all he can give her.

Carmen searches his eyes and face. Through his mask, deep down where her powers should reside, she feels him. A trickle. More than what she's felt in over a year after she cut herself off from her powers. But she sees him.

"I do not fear you," she whispers, stroking up his jaw. "My knight."

Alanzo, ever so slightly, becomes less rigid in his shoulders. He reaches up, touching her hand against his jaw. The stony wall upon his face softens next, melting quickly under her gaze.

"I love you...my life," he says, clutching her hand.

"I love you, my knight. Let us continue searching for our home."

Hands remaining wrapped around the other, they walk into the middle of the meadow. His wings shimmer into existence, flaring out behind him and stretching his muscles. More light glows from the sun rising into the day, clouds separating as the storm finally passes. Adjusting their supplies and pack, Alanzo then takes Carmen back into his arms as she holds onto him. Once secured, his wings beat down once to fly up into the clouds and away from the flooded woods and lingering scent of charred iron.

Chapter Six

"I've loved the stars too fondly to be fearful of the night"
- Galileo Galilei

Late afternoon looms before them as they fly through the skies, coming up over hills and into a heavily wooded area. Alanzo circles around, searching through brush as he moves them over to the edge of the forest. He lands easily upon his feet, settling back onto the ground before he allows his wings to disappear. This time, he lets Carmen down from his arms before she can protest. Her light smile makes his heart flutter as he takes her hand, leading her towards the forest where he'd seen a small clearing from the sky.

The journey had been cold in the beginning, chilling him to the bone from the damp clothes. They'd dried once he found some sunlight to fly within for a time, warming both of them as he searched through the terrain. A careful eye he kept upon their surroundings below, noting villages and towns he'd once been through. Many to avoid due to the overpopulation of humans and other beings not trustworthy to remain near.

For him, they were still too close to their old village. Too close to betrayal of their families. His gut urged him to continue; keep looking.

"Did you find a cave?" She asks.

"No. We'll sleep under the stars tonight. The skies are clear, and storms have moved on."

"Why do you not want to travel during the night?"

"Other Paranormal beings may be traveling near and will be awake. I do not wish to cross their paths unless necessary." He glimpses over at her, and she tilts her head at him. "Easier to evade and better to see the terrain as well in the daylight."

Her response is a small nod, following him into the forest.

They weave through the trees as sunlight bounces through the branches and leaves. The rain has come through here as well, leaving small puddles and dampness behind, but nowhere near the destruction of where they'd journeyed from. Chirping of birds fill the air, along with the chittering of animals as they rustle through the leaves. They continue towards the clearing Alanzo had found, one where they could rest. It's not long before they do, coming upon the tiny area where a couple of trees have fallen. Patches of dirt are scattered around, which will make it easier to build a small fire safely and the fallen trees could be sat upon. Alanzo glimpses up at the trees surrounding, noticing the strong branches.

"Here, we'll stay. We can hang the damp clothing and blankets to dry near the fire," Alanzo instructs, tugging the pack off his back. Carmen nods, taking it from him to begin hanging the last of the wet cloth to dry.

They set up camp, putting together a fire that's not too close to the hanging fabric to not catch fire. In a few hours, they should be more than dry to sleep comfortably. A quick meal is made of the bread and dried meat they have, including some berries Carmen foraged while Alanzo collected wood. It's about an hour before sunset when they settle in for their simple meal, darkening orange and red painting the sky past the treetops.

Carmen lays her cloak over a log, sitting down to face the warming fire. Alanzo does a final check of their surroundings, walking around their small campsite as he searches the dense woods. He looks up a moment, noting the clearing is smaller than he thought from above. He won't be able to fly out of here, branches reaching too far in and closely. They'd have to walk back to the edge of the forest. Concern stirs in his chest, whilst hoping there won't be a reason to flee quickly. His eyes flick to where they came, remembering the path they took.

Carmen watches him as he prowls around the clearing before finally joining her upon the log. Instead of facing the fire like her, he sits to look out at the forest instead. They sit side by side in the silence. She watches the flames dance and spark over the wood, while he watches the noisy, darkening forest around them.

Night falls quietly and slowly, taking away the last of the sunlight. Soon, it is just the firelight illuminating the forest, casting long and moving shadows.

"When will we know we've found our home?" She asks gently, moving her hand to lay upon his. It's warm underneath her fingertips.

"We shall know." His answer has her looking over at him with a tender expression. He returns it in kind.

"What will you do, my knight?" Her voice mingles with the pop of the firewood. Alanzo raises a brow at her in question. "You've been traveling for so long, across the world and into different kingdoms and nations. What if you grow tired of the same place? No adventure?"

"There was no adventure to be had while you were gone." His voice rasps, turning back towards the silent woods. His eyes become distant. "A home is what I desire. Crave. With you, my life."

Carmen gazes upon the fire, curling her fingers around his, whispering, "Neither of us met adventure."

"Do you want it, my heart? Adventure?" Alanzo asks.

"I am too frightened of the world for it."

Alanzo turns his hand over, weaving his fingers with hers to clutch her hand. Neither of them speaks as he senses her heightened emotions. Fear, sorrow, and trickling of shame that brings a heaviness to his heart. Once more he wishes he could tap into that part of his powers, to soothe her and to take the pain she carries.

He cannot. Not anymore.

Alanzo could only bring fear and destruction now; no longer an incubus who created joy and happiness.

He stares out at the woods, wishing it would not always be like this. Perhaps, time would change them once again, and he yearned it would be in this new home they'd find. A place to heal and love, find faith in the world again. Hope in happiness.

"Living life with you, my heart..." he begins, eyes flicking over the rustling leaves, "...shall be adventure enough for me. Let it be quiet. Let it be simple. It shall be all what I need without the turmoil of the world around us. As long as I never have to walk or fly across this world in the loneliness that once shrouded me, you are all I need. I was not created for adventure; I was created to love you. For the world frightens me without you in it."

Tears gather in Carmen's eyes, blinking them away as they fall down her cheeks. She turns to stare upon the profile of Alanzo's face—her Mate. He the one who destroyed so much to find her, including fragments of himself that may never return. He was not the same incubus she had fallen in love with, long gone was the carefree and joyous manner he once lived life. Alanzo was once known as the incubus for loving the daylight and the wonders of the world, curious of its inventions and creating friendships with any walk of life whether it was Paranormal beings or human. He was so open-hearted and loving, naïve perhaps, but it was out of the want to bring joy to the world. *That* Alanzo had craved adventure with such openness as he used to speak of discovering the world around them.

Who sat beside her now was still her Alanzo, her Mate, yet he was not.

This version of him was reserved and overly thoughtful. This Alanzo did not crave for friendships as he had or speak of hopeful discovery. They may be traveling in the daylight for protection, but he did not revel in it as he had before. His words were more precise, yet they haven't fully lost the passion behind them. Not to her. The biggest change was the emotions he carried within his gaze. Anger. Weariness. Exhaustion. All of them lingering, never truly leaving him. Even while they lived outside their old village, he was tense and ever-watchful as he had been when they traveled by ship back to Italy. As he was right now, a forever sentry, waiting for danger.

The Alanzo she had fallen in love with was gone.

Then again, she wasn't the same either. The succubus she once was had been destroyed.

He had found no adventure traveling the world, while she found none chained inside caverns. All she had known for years was pain and terror. The cruelty of the world was shown to her, opening like a chasm that threatened to drown her in torment. He was no longer the naïve, happy incubus and she was no longer the open-hearted, smiling succubus that was once adored.

Neither of them would be that again.

Their pasts would remain in their past, perhaps one day fully forgotten.

Yet, his words of finding adventure in a simple life simmered hope inside her. They were not those beings anymore, but they could be something new. She wanted, no...ached to be something new, and not this shell of a being she once was.

Swallowing hard, Carmen pulls her hand from his to gently cup his face. He turns his attention to her, violet eyes hardened and protective. Her thumb strokes over his cheek as she begins to lean her face closer to his.

"Carmen," he rasps, almost a plea upon his lips.

Keeping her hand firm upon his cheek, her forehead touches his as she breathes in his faint scent. It was hidden under the aroma of his powers that followed him, but she could sense it—cinnamon and sweetened smoke.

A memory flickers, reminding her that's what his powers would smell like when he calmed her in the past. Or whenever he helped provide warmth and love. A scent she could barely touch within him anymore, as if he'd lost that part of him, too.

Closing her eyes, she breathes in the hints of it. Alanzo does the same, for he could sense the faint aroma of her powers that she locked away. For a moment, he could practically taste it—sweet cherry blossoms. A name he could not place upon it until he found the real tree in its native country, haunted by the perfume until he found her. Much like his, it did not return fully, but the traces were there.

They remain frozen in time, quiet as the fire burns and crackles.

Pulled by a love that transcended past pain and distance, Carmen slowly dips her head downward. Alanzo goes completely still as her lips brush over his, causing his body to shiver as he inhales sharply at the very light touch. Again, she does it, something igniting in his chest to taste what he has not for almost seven years. Her tender touch is delicate as if in fear it could shatter underneath their fingertips. Carmen's own body trembles as she holds his face still, pulling away. Her eyes open, finding Alanzo's closed as tears begin to trickle down his cheeks.

"Alanzo," she murmurs affectionately. "My Alanzo."

His watery eyes open, and his chest squeezes. Carmen's expression is open and loving. Carefully, he reaches up to caress her cheek, feeling the softness of her skin against his fingertips. With a simple nod from her, Alanzo leans in and kisses her.

The touch is not as light as before like they were tempting waters with one's finger before jumping in. Now, it is a delicate and soft touch as their lips press against the other. Neither of them taste the same, and yet they do as if remembering a past dream. A deep understanding of adoration reaches far into the crevices to the fragments of them that have been locked away. An elation of hope and love.

Both of them shiver lightly before pulling away at the same time.

Their eyes meet, embers reflecting in their gazes.

Their second first kiss.

Foreheads touching, they lean into the other as silent tears fall from them both. Shadows play upon their features, the forest almost becoming completely silent around them. Slowly, they both breathe in a hint of the other's fragrance they once memorized so long ago to keep from shattering while separated.

Carmen's voice cracks through the quiet, "Will it...will it become easier?"

"Yes," he answers. "I believe we will make it so."

"You always were a dreamer."

"Not as I used to be."

"No," she murmurs, moving enough to see his gaze. "Your dreams are different. That is all. But you, my knight, still are. For only you would envision a valley for us, complete with a garden."

Alanzo shifts where he sits, turning around to face the fire alongside her. His arm goes around her shoulder, nestling her into his side as she presses her face into the crook of his shoulder.

"I will help you tend it and bake as well." He says softly.

A bit of laughter leaves her, and he lights up inside at the soft sound. "You will burn the bread."

"Just a little."

"You can help me harvest the garden."

Alanzo settles his head against hers, holding her protectively. "Whatever you ask of me, I shall do."

Carmen touches his chest, placing her hand over where his heart is. His own falls over hers, holding it there as it beats within his chest loudly.

"All I ask is for you to love me," she murmurs.

"Until the end of our days, into the afterlife, my beautiful heart."

Chapter Seven

"Nature repairs one thing from another and allows nothing to be born without the aid of another's death."
- Lucretius

Eerie silence wakes Alanzo first.

A stillness settling upon the forest as he snaps his eyes open, rising from his sleeping position next to Carmen. The birds are gone. There's only a light breeze, rustling the leaves as he searches the area around them. His powers flow out of him, searching for the disruption and it quickly finds the wrongness. A hardness forms in his gut as he gently wakens Carmen as quietly as he can.

"We need to leave."

"Alanzo, what—"

"Shh. If the birds leave, then we leave."

He stands, pulling down the dried clothing from their branches. Carmen quickly helps him gather the rest of the supplies as he scatters the embers from the campfire. He could use it but destroying the forest would be a worse issue. The ash covers the dirt, mixing together as Alanzo pulls out his sword.

It's barely been a few minutes when Alanzo senses a shift in the wind. A drift of the wrongness closing in. His powers ease further out, touching upon the oily feeling of decay as he recoils.

"Stop," he whispers, holding his hand up to pause Carmen's movement. She goes still from his quiet command, eyes wide as she watches him.

Alanzo waits.

Still no birds sing. Nor the faint chirp of crickets as dawn creeps over the horizon. It's faint light barely giving enough to illuminate the shadows that persist through the darkened woods.

The breeze stops.

Alanzo flicks his gaze up, assessing again if he could fly out through the trees. Determination sets inside him—survival. If he tried, he could endanger them both and ruin his wings for days before they heal. He can't chance it with how early they've begun their journey.

Wildlife completely ceases around them as Carmen steps closer, clutching his arm as he looks towards where the worst of the wrongness hails. Decay.

Alanzo's muscles tense, preparing for the threat that he knows is looming. His powers flourish around him, hoping to deter the creatures that are coming to hunt. Except, he knows it won't last long.

There's a reason he's steered clear of these diseased beings for so long.

The oily, rotten feeling of rot scrapes over his powers finding multiple living beings. A hoard. Worse if it's a whole hive.

Without a word, he trickles his powers to hopefully distract the coming threat as he gestures for Carmen to finish packing. She does so diligently and silently, and he pulls the pack onto her shoulders. Taking her hand, he leads her back the way they had come as he slides his sword out.

"Run for the edge of the forest," he commands.

Carmen's blue eyes widen in fear, her own terror now seeping into him. It does not deter him but bolsters his powers at the taste of it. He lightly pushes her forward.

"Run, my love. *Now*."

She takes off through the trees as he follows behind her. He does not look behind, feeling the beings closing in as he hears the snap of twigs and breaking of branches. The silence of the forest now filled with cracking and rustling of dragging feet. Watery breaths as if they've drowned in muddied water.

His powers pulse out of him, slamming into a decaying mind of one of the beings chasing them. Alanzo finally can physically smell them as they close in, stopping suddenly and swiping his sword up as he turns. Dark, browning blood spurts onto the ground as he slices through the ghoul. Their grey skin and tattered orange hair flinging back. He quickly thrusts his powers into its mind, breaking it as it screams and falls. Another snapping noise comes from behind him as he spins upon his heel, blade quickly decapitating the next one.

There's a scream in the distance and Alanzo snarls, knowing they've come upon a hive of Feral ghouls. The leader isn't much further behind.

He starts running again, faster than before as he shoves past the branches and shrubbery. His powers lash out, searching for Carmen when he hears her shriek. Terror grips him, threatening to shove him under with despair that he shouldn't have let her go far. Shouldn't have let her out of his sight.

Another scream echoes as he races out of the forest and sees her not far on the ground. She scrambles back from the two ghouls chasing after her. Their dead skin dropping off their bodies as they fight each other, wanting her for their own. One bite, and there will be no saving her from transforming into one of them. Sprinting, he flips his sword and throws it like a javelin. It soars through the air, whistling through the lack of wind before it lands directly through the head of one ghoul. It convulses as it falls to the ground, the other stopping their attack to stare at their companion.

Again, a screech echoes from the distance as the standing ghoul looks towards where it comes. It turns to attack Alanzo next, but he swiftly grabs his sword and the blade cuts through their neck. Their head rolls away as Alanzo reaches for Carmen, wings shimmering into existence as he looks to her with hardened eyes.

"Did they bite you?"

"No," she breathes out, clutching him as she trembles violently. "No, no."

There's shaking in the forest line, and suddenly a burst of movement comes. Over a dozen ghouls breach the edge of the shadowed forest. Some of them shrieking at the light that reaches above the horizon.

"Around me!" He orders as she jumps into his arms, limbs wrapped around his body as one of his arms go around her torso. His other hand grips his sword harshly, brandishing it as his wings beat down to propel them into the air.

They leave the ground moments before two of the ghouls can grab them. Their shrieks ripping through the eerie quiet, replacing it with horror.

Carmen watches below as Alanzo flies further into the sky, far away from the ghouls pouring out of the forest. Her eyes flick to the edge of the trees, noticing one walk out in such wrath, screeching in such a way that hurts her ears. Carmen buries her face into Alanzo's shoulder as he flies further up into the clouds, and then hovers in the air as he glances down at the nightmarish scene.

"What is wrong with them? Why are they—?" She rasps, voice swallowed up in the wind, unable to pull her eyes away from the Paranormal beings that begin to fight each other. They tug and pull, while some shriek at the daylight that begins to cover the earth. A few run back into the shadowed forest.

"Feral ghouls," Alanzo answers. "A hive as well."

His wings beat down, turning his body away from the horrific scene. Carmen clutches his body, feeling the wind upon her back as he steers them through the sky. Those shrieks will haunt her, along with many other nightmares and memories that follow in her wake.

Alanzo searches, finding a hill away from the danger they had escaped. He eases them down, mostly landing gently upon his feet as he lets Carmen stand.

"What are Feral ghouls?" Carmen asks, wrapping her arms around herself as Alanzo sets to clean his blade.

"A sickness comes over them," he answers. "They lose all sense of self and the last of their emotions. Their Hive Mind, the one who created them, is all who can control them. If they are all as such, then it is them who is most effected."

"They have been living in Italy? All this time?"

"It is rare to happen. They are not created...normally as such."

Carmen runs her hands over her arms, shivering at the thought of them almost biting her and turning her into such a being. Her stomach twists in worry as she looks out where they'd flown from.

"It is harder to use my powers on them," Alanzo continues, finishing cleaning his sword as he puts it away. "They do not think or feel like other beings anymore. Not even as *ghouls* anymore. Their fear and anger are different. For they do not fear most monsters."

Alanzo's voice is a rasp as he takes the pack off Carmen's shoulders, putting it upon his.

She searches his face, weary as realization settles upon her. "You have fought them before."

"Unfortunately, yes." Alanzo meets her gaze, his own eyes still hardened with determination and pulsing with territorial need. He brings his powers in, realizing they have been lashing out around him in want to destroy and cause horror. "Where the sickness comes from, originates, I do not know. I do not believe anyone knows. And it is something that can happen to any Paranormal being."

Carmen gasps, touching her throat as her breath shakes. Alanzo takes her hand, clutching it as he makes her look into his eyes. "It is not contagious, that I do know."

"How do you know?"

"A friend. Who tried to study why some Paranormal beings become Feral...why they lose their senses. And this was the first time I have encountered them in Italy."

"Where...where have you seen it before?"

"Further north, near Bohemia. I've heard stories of this sickness appearing near the Mutapa Empire as well." Carmen looks at him in confusion, not knowing where he speaks of. "Much further south of the land you were held prisoner in."

She nods her head, breathing a bit better as the scent of decaying flesh leaves her nostrils.

"It can happen anywhere?" She asks.

"I believe so. Perhaps, one day, it shall be learned why it occurs." He turns his gaze towards where they were, pursing his lips with concentration. "Many a story I've heard of mad kings and monarchs, I've wondered if that is what occurs with humans and Paranormals alike who start wars."

"Why?"

"It is easier to imagine cruelty coming from a disease than from one's heart." He exhales heavily, not focusing upon the subject in his mind that has long been discussed many times with another. "We shall be more careful where we camp. We came across a hungry group is all."

"Ghouls don't eat—"

"The Feral ones do. If they are starved enough." He does not pull his eyes away from where the faint screeching echoes. "Their undead side takes over, my heart. They are not ghouls or Paranormal beings anymore, but something else entirely."

"The same happens to...*other* Paranormal beings who get this sickness?"

Alanzo adjusts the straps of his pack, making certain it is secure as he rolls back his shoulders to ready himself to travel.

"Vampires become more bloodthirsty. Werewolves become like rapid dogs, unsatisfied with any bone they find. Incubi and succubi resort to our most primal forms of emotion." Carmen stares at him in disbelief, unknowing such a thing existed in this world. Along with every other horror out there, and now this? A disease that could take away a Paranormal being's benevolence and their intelligence.

Alanzo brings his hand upon her cheek, having her worried eyes meet his.

"They are not unstoppable," he says softly. "Harder to fight, even with what I am able. It is difficult to find their fear, so it is smart to run when we can. But it is a rare sickness. We are safe."

"For how long?" She whispers.

"While you are with me, you always are." He strokes his thumb over her cheek, and then bends to pick her up into his arms. Carmen's goes around his shoulders, holding him close. "I will keep you safe from harm, my love. Through any threat, that sickness or any other."

"I know." She lays her head on his shoulder, tugging on the belief that he will uphold that promise. For the other outcome was far too terrible to think of.

They launch into the sky as the sun rises, daylight streaming through the clouds in brilliant orange and yellow light.

Chapter Eight

"The noblest pleasure is the joy of understanding."
– Leonardo da Vinci

Two days have passed since the encounter with the Feral ghouls. Alanzo has barely stopped flying and moving, unnerved by almost being run upon by the hive that discovered them. He flies hard and fast, searching for what could be their home. Valleys, farmland, forests...none that they come across is secluded enough from the towns and people he knows are too close. Although they've traveled far from their village, setting a long distance between them, nothing has settled within his gut that it was theirs to call home.

Find it. The compulsion ripples through him as they soar through the skies. Carmen's eyes are closed as he flies as he glances down upon her restful face. *Find it. Keep her safe.*

The craving to protect her gnaws at his core as visions of fire, storms, and oceans cloud his mind. The past weighs heavy upon him as he continues his search over the land.

Find it.

The words echo much like the ones which had spurred him on for years—*find her. Find HER.*

Sudden melancholy swarms Alanzo, clutching his Mate closer

to remind himself he has her. She is not gone. The hope he once had that was barely a burning ember was now a small flame in his chest.

His thoughts wander, attempting to escape the barrage of images of the past and the emotions they drag behind. He hears her words, telling him he's still a dreamer.

Was he?

Alanzo turns his body downward, noticing the beginning descent of the sun as he bursts through the clouds. Below, he sees farmland along with vineyards, hills filled with growing grape vines. There's a village not far from where he soars, noticing people in their wagons and working the fields. He continues downward, aiming for a hill that's near an orchard that is out of sight from the farmers.

He lands a bit less softly on his feet than usual, exhaustion looming as he keeps himself standing with Carmen in his arms. Everything in him aches from traveling and moving for days on end.

He inhales a long breath, looking out at the hillside filled with trees and growing fruit. Longing hits him, wanting sooner for them to have their own orchard of growing fruits. Their own place to farm and harvest fresh food for themselves. A simple life.

Carmen stirs in his arms, eyes blinking open as she realizes they are not flying anymore. She eases upward in his hold, and he allows her to stand upon her own feet. He does not say anything, while his wings shimmer into non-existence once more as he holds back a groan from the ache throughout his back. He reminds himself he's been through worse; flown in harsher weather and for longer hours.

This was nothing. He would not stop or falter until they found their home. *This was nothing*, he repeated in his head.

"My knight?" Carmen asks, touching his arm. "Are you well?"

"I am." He pulls the pack off, and then his sword to lay beneath some trees that overlook the grove.

"You do not...*feel* well." She presses further, looking over his rigid body as concern begins to fill her. Had something occurred while she slept? Perhaps she could convince him this time to sleep, while she played sentry this night.

"I am yearning for your bread," he says, giving her a very faint smile. His eyes glisten a little, glancing over her. "Hunger is what plagues me, my love. That is all. Let us eat."

"And stay here for the night? To rest?"

"We must—"

"Wherever our home is, it shall not disappear if we arrive in days or weeks," she says, laying her hand gently upon his to stop him.

Alanzo peers over his shoulder to her, and then releases a sigh. Unable to argue with her, he nods as they lay out their blanket. Carmen pulls out what food they have left, which is not much as she purses her lips at the short supply. She knows that he knows, which perhaps is why he is reluctant in pausing in their journey.

For more provisions, he'd either must hunt or venture into a village or town. Giuseppe had given them some coins, enough to buy more food and possibly a night at an inn if they wanted. She looks over her shoulder at him as he sits, resting his back against the trunk of the wider tree. Its branches swish above as a breeze comes, warmth spreading over the hill as the clouds move and give way for more of the sunlight.

His eyes close, leaning his head back.

Deep within her core, Carmen knows he will not stop until they are safe. He shall fly himself ragged into the ground, until his wings become frail. He had done it before while searching for her. She did not know how much he broke himself to find her. Worry begins to simmer that he shall do it again. Break himself not in finding her this time, but a home for them.

Her eyes peer up at the bright sky, flicking over the peaceful clouds. White and puffy, shadows of blue over their curves as the sunlight pours through them. She wishes upon a silent hope they find what they need. To find the very place Alanzo dreams of and to give, perhaps, a piece of him back by realizing his dreams can be real. Good dreams.

Let me see him again. Her thoughts venture out into the vast unknown skies.

Carmen goes back to setting out the food, what's left of the dried meat and hardened bread from being within the bag. She sits beside Alanzo, noticing he's swiftly fallen asleep. A soft smile rises upon her face, reaching over to caress the side of his cheek. He does not stir. His expression relaxed.

She starts to grab one of the dried meats, when she looks upon the orchard they're resting nearby. Standing, she ventures closer as she notices in the distance of human workers harvesting the fruit. Wagons are pulled through lanes, and she can see a wall for the farm or village that takes care of the land. Glancing over her shoulder, Carmen sees he is still asleep. Briefly, she looks around for any danger, but discovers nothing aside from more trees.

Her steps are quiet, exploring further as she walks through the fluttering tall grass as a breeze passes through. She comes to the edge of the orchard, looking up at the trees and a sense of relief fills her. Pears. Easily, she reaches up and plucks a ripe fruit from the branch. She smells it, finding the sweet scent of the fruit. Holding her skirt out, she starts to collect more fruit from the trees. Soon she has a handful of pears, and a true warm smile spreads over her face.

All of a sudden, there's a shout in the distance. Her gaze snaps up, smile gone as she looks down the lane of the orchard. She gets ready to run and take her stolen fruit back to her Mate but stops.

There, quite far, is a small child. A human child. They look toward her, head tilting to the side in wonder. Swallowing hard, she waits to see if they call for their family. For anyone. No noise comes from the small boy. Instead, he raises his hand in a small wave.

Warmth fills her chest, easing into her bones. Gently, she raises her free hand, waving back to the young one. A grin breaks out over his face, wide and carefree. Her hand falls when there's a call in the distance.

"Riccardo!"

The boy turns, looking over his shoulder toward the voice. He looks back at Carmen, still grinning and waves once more before he dashes through the trees.

Her smile returns, even when she realizes she must leave before anyone else may stride through the trees, and it may not be a curious boy. Keeping the fruit close to her, she rushes away from the orchard as she makes her way back up the hill towards their small camp. Nearing the top, she arrives in time as Alanzo jostles awake from his sleep. His eyes snap open, finding her walking back to him.

He starts to stand, worry etched upon his face, but she shakes her head at him fondly.

"I am well, my knight," she says, holding out the part of her skirt where the fruit is. "I found fruit."

A grin almost forms upon his face as he settles back where he is. Carmen comes over to the blanket, sitting down alongside him to show him her spoils. She takes a pear, holding it out for him. Those violet eyes of his soften with appreciation, taking the fresh fruit from her grasp to bite into. Before she grabs one for herself, her eyes pause upon his mouth. The movement of his jaw and the small bit of juice that trickles from his lips. His throat bobbing as he swallows and takes another bite.

Blinking quickly, she looks away as she takes a pear and bites into one herself.

Alanzo relishes in the sweet taste of the pear, a reprieve from the salty dried meat and plain bread of late. The ripe fruit is soft and juicy. He looks up mid-bite, his gaze falling upon Carmen as she hums eating her own. Joy flits over her face as she swallows the sweet fruit and takes another bite. Easy warmth settles into his chest as he finishes his, grabbing another as she does. Their fingers brush upon the other, and they share reserved smiles.

Halfway through the pears she collected, they stop to save them for another meal. Carmen settles beside Alanzo, both now leaning against the trunk of the tree as they sit. In the distance, there's the sound of voices shouting and then a child's laughter. Carmen wonders if it was the boy...Riccardo.

She leans her head against his shoulder, sighing gently. "Alanzo?"

"Yes, my heart?"

"Do...do you want children?"

He does not go still beneath her touch, but his breath does catch a moment at the question he was not prepared for. He stares out at the orchard, hearing the faint sound of the child's laughter. It felt foreign to hear. A sound he has become unaccustomed to.

"Do you want them, my love?"

"That is not an answer, my knight."

"I shall not be the one carrying them if we do," he says, smoothing a hand along her thigh.

Carmen's mouth lifts a little in a smile, appreciation growing as she keeps her head against his shoulder. "One day," she answers.

He continues to stare out at the farmland before them. Thoughts running across his mind, coupled with fear and discernment.

"What is it?" She asks. "Do you not?"

"That is not...what I want."

"You don't want children?"

"No," he takes her hand, bringing it up gently towards his lips. His mouth presses against her knuckles tenderly, barely a kiss upon them. "I do, but I am afraid."

"Why?"

"That...I shall not protect them well enough. From the horrors of this world or worse to lose them to it." He peers over at her, violet eyes meeting her cobalt blue gaze. "They would be a piece of you, and if anything happened to them...I would struggle to exist in shame and despair. I could fail...again."

She watches him carefully. "You do not believe you would be a good father?"

"I do not know."

"Do you fear losing me?"

"Every moment I breathe."

"Yet, you love me and do not leave. You found me." She sits up straighter, tilting her head at him. "You would be a marvelous father. Loving. Protective. Kind."

His face pinches together, averting his eyes from hers. "I have been a dangerous monster for years, my heart. I am not certain I possess those qualities which you recall of a past life long gone."

A warm gale passes through, ruffling his hair upon his forehead. The quiet surrounds them, until Carmen says, "You would never be a monster to them."

Alanzo brings his attention back to her, face falling a little.

"For you have never been a monster to me. The Alanzo that is before me now *does* possess the qualities I speak of. For I have witnessed them this past fortnight." She smiles, tightening her fingers around his. "You would protect and love them as you have with me. You would not fail in that."

His gaze softens as she brings their joined hands up, kissing his knuckles next in a delicate manner.

"You would be a wonderful mother," he murmurs low. "Patient. Loving. Nurturing."

She smiles delicately.

"Then one day...we could have our own," she whispers.

Alanzo looks down upon their hands, and then back out to the scenery. The breeze returns, rustling some of Carmen's hair. It is a warm out with spring in full force, but she shivers a moment from the light chill. Alanzo tenderly pulls her back to him, partially settling her over his torso as he wraps his arms around her. His warm body seeps into hers as she lays her head upon his chest.

"When this world is safer, my heart," he whispers in a rasp. "What it is now, I do not...wish for them to witness what it is. When we are stronger and can provide a home that is warm, welcoming, and it shall be their haven. When we have..."

"Healed more."

He lays his head back, holding her in his arms as a reminder that she is here. Their journey still lays far before them, but she is with him.

"Yes," he murmurs. "One day."

"One day," she whispers. The sun begins to set, casting long shadows as they remain there in silence and hope.

Carmen hears the child's laughter in the distance and can almost imagine it being her own son one day.

Chapter Nine

"There is no greater sorrow then to recall our times of joy in wretchedness."
– Dante Alighieri

They are out of food.

The pears Carmen gathered when they had stayed near the orchard had not lasted long. Soon after, their bag of provisions became empty. Alanzo knew it was coming but had hoped they would've found a place to call their home before their bag was bare. Or perhaps a good area where he could hunt. Except, the rain had returned, drenching the hills of Italy making all animals scarce. Their final option would have to be taken.

Dusk had barely passed, rain sprinkling down over the dirt road outside the small town they've come upon. There's a wall around it, sandy stone that stands tall hiding away the thatched roofs of the buildings within.

Carmen and Alanzo stand under a tree, hiding from the falling rain, not far from the gate of the town. Alanzo adjusts her cloak, pulling the hood over her head to completely hide her horns and hair. He does the same, disappearing into the shadow of his cloak as he glances at the gate again. There has been no movement to show if it is a Paranormal town or human. He could sense with his powers different kinds of beings, giving him a clue that it could be one of the few towns where all live peacefully.

"Will anyone recognize you?" Carmen's voice is quiet.

The larger concern for Alanzo.

They were far from the shores of the ocean and the red sea, but he knew stories have traveled far of his deeds. His damnation from the world.

"No one knows my true identity," he says, taking her arm to keep her close as they venture towards the gate. "We are simply a couple traveling north."

She remains close as they get to the gate, approaching a few guards. Alanzo takes a moment to ask them for the closest inn that would have rooms or food. They point down the path where there's little light, a few lamps flickering against the drizzling rain. Giving thanks they continue and come to the inn the guards had indicated. Quietly, Alanzo opens the door into the building.

Inside there are mostly humans, seated at tables and a couple at the bar along the backside of the tavern floor. Within moments, Alanzo senses the other Paranormals in the room as some glimpse towards them. A couple werewolves, an incubus, a gargoyle, and two shifters. A wide array of Paranormal beings he has not seen in some time.

Quietly they walk towards the bar, keeping their hoods up. Carmen's hand squeezes Alanzo's, refusing to let go as awareness pulses over her. She attempts to hide her worry within the new space and people around them. Her eyes dart towards some of the humans who watch them as they weave through the busy establishment.

They approach the bar where a woman with blonde hair twisted up greets them. She cleans a glass, setting it aside and gives a weary smile. "Evening, how may I help you?"

"Do you have a room open?" Alanzo asks.

"We do. A single bed."

"That shall do. We are needing of food as well until we can replenish our supplies in the morning unless there is a night market."

She shakes her head, turning to open a cabinet and pulls out a key. "Only day markets. There are not enough Paranormals living here to have nightly markets. You'll have to wait until break of day."

Alanzo nods once, assuming that already from the lack of trading posts and shops opened as they arrived. Rain or not, it was quiet outside.

"We have mushroom soup and bread if you want to eat."

"We do. Yes." Alanzo glances over at Carmen who remains close to his side, eyes peering out at the small crowd of people within the inn. "A bath as well if you can provide it. We've been traveling for quite some time."

"There's a tub in your room. I'll have someone fill it while you two eat. Yes?" Alanzo nods, pulling out coins to pay the keeper. She takes it, sliding the key over to him. "It'll be the room down the left, two doors down on the right. Sit where you like for now. I'll bring out the food."

"Thank you."

Alanzo leads them away towards a table near the wall. He sits with his back against the hard surface, pulling the other chair closer for Carmen to be within arm's length. Slowly, he pulls down the hood of his cloak as he sets aside their bag as they wait for their food. Peering over her shoulder a moment at the other patrons, Carmen reaches up to drag the damp hood of her cloak down. Weariness floods Alanzo as he watches her, eyes flicking towards the Paranormals at the other tables.

The humans pay them no attention, staying to themselves in conversations along with the werewolves and shifters at their prospective seats. There's some grumbling, perhaps from those playing a game or from lack of drink as one of the werewolves stand. Their deep grey skin appears darker in the shadows of the lamplights, sauntering over to the bar where the woman, inn keeper more likely, takes his empty glass to refill.

A pulse flickers in the air, and he feels Carmen stiffen in her seat as she keeps her gaze down at the table. Alanzo's violet eyes quickly move to where he feels the shift, someone's powers far lesser than his, stretching out across the room. His hardened gaze comes to the table where the incubus sits, who is across from one of the gargoyles here. Their blue eyes meet his, suspicion rising in them as he flits his attention to Carmen. The lines upon the light rue shade of the incubus' skin deepen over their forehead, eyes narrowing.

Briefly, Alanzo follows his gaze to Carmen. Her short, cropped hair is mussed around her ears from being under her hood and the wet weather. The sheen it used to have years ago has not returned, now mostly a flattened black color. Hands shaking, she smooths some of the strands back behind her ears as she averts her gaze from the other incubus.

A small snarl rises from Alanzo's throat, eyes beginning to glow as his powers seep out of him. He feels it wrap around the incubus, warning sinking into the being's mind as he easily finds their emotions—disgust. Repulsion.

Short hair upon a succubus means disgrace to their community. A sign of exile and dishonor amongst their kind. An old unspoken rule that Alanzo has long hated. He had watched many beings lose their hair due to slavery while kept as prisoners. Some ripped out by their own hands or cut from their captors. If it had grown closer to her shoulders or if she wore a head covering, there perhaps would be less of their staring.

Carmen's hand reaches up, about to pull the hood back over her head to hide beneath it. Alanzo stops her quietly, taking her hand as she looks to him with her large unsure eyes. His thumb caresses over her wrist, keeping his violet gaze with hers. While doing so, his powers prick into the other incubus' mind. He can feel the jolt from them and the fear, swarming under the surface as there's a gasp from across the room. It's faint, only for Alanzo's ears to hear of his next victim. The very idea of ripping apart another's mind ripples under his skin, the monster inside him wanting release to destroy and cause mayhem. Terror.

His eyes flick past Carmen to the incubus, who is stone still. He no longer looks at Carmen, gaze now wide with fear as his eyes remain fixed upon the ground. His friend, the gargoyle, frowns deeply and then brings their attention to Alanzo. They're next for his prey as Alanzo easily moves past the defenses of the gargoyle's mind, which is not difficult to overcome. They become stark still, body rigid as Alanzo easily holds both firmly in his grasp with the swirling of terror creeping along the crevices of their minds.

"Alanzo." Carmen's faint voice pulls Alanzo back to the present. "Not here."

He flicks his gaze to her, face impassive with no proof of what he is doing to the Paranormal beings across the room. Not letting them go, he stands and gestures for her to do the same. Grabbing their pack, he tells the inn keeper they'll take their meal up in their room. She simply nods her head, unknowing what is happening to a couple of her patrons.

Alanzo guides Carmen to the stairs, leading her up first before his powers twisting in the other minds is slipped away. The incubus and gargoyle jolt back to the reality of where they are, shivering and talking low with the other. Neither of them looks towards Alanzo or Carmen, nor the table where they once sat.

Alanzo's face is emotionless, only the glowing of his eyes remains as a remnant of what he's done as he completely wipes away their presence from the room below. They are but a faded memory to the patrons as they reach the second story of the building, going down the short hall to find their room. They find their room door open, where someone brings in a couple pails of hot water, nodding at them before pouring it into the tub in the back of the room. It's a simple space with a singular wide bed, table and chair, and small table next to the bedside. The human filling the tub, provides one more nod before leaving and shuts the door behind themselves.

"What did you—"

"Made them forget their fear," Alanzo answers before Carmen can finish her question. She watches him as she sets aside their bag upon the bed. He then looks out the window, rain streaking down the glass barely seen from the small bit of light from the lamp burning in the corner.

Alanzo undoes his belt, beginning to set his sword aside.

"Take a bath, my love. Rest."

"You are the one who should rest, my knight," she murmurs, pulling her cloak off carefully. He takes it along with his, hanging them up to dry upon the hooks near the room's entrance.

"I shall be fine." He goes to her and easily cups her cheeks, wiping away a stray tear from what he knows happened below. "Unless you think I smell."

Her mouth pulls up in almost a smirk, and then delicately shakes her head. Alanzo leans in quietly, placing his lips upon her forehead as his hand caresses her hair affectionately.

"Bathe, my heart. While the water is warm."

At that moment, stepping apart there's a knock at the door. Carmen jumps, attention moving to the noise as Alanzo remains stoic. He gestures for her to go to the other side, and then carefully opens the door. A human stands upon the threshold, holding a wide tray with bowls of food on it. Alanzo opens the door further, nodding his gratitude as he takes the tray from their hands. They flinch when his fingers brush over theirs, apparent curious fear flashing over their expression. The young man swallows hard, stepping back and dips his head down.

Alanzo watches him disappear down the hall, rounding the corner for the kitchen service stairs. Not as mixed with different beings here than he thought. Or the incubus below was a newcomer to the town. The werewolves seemed quite at home below, as did the shifters. Questions rise within Alanzo as he steps back, bringing the food into the room and sets it aside, and then finally locks the door for the night. Carmen quietly pulls her blouse off and then her skirt, along with her other undergarments.

Turning around, the questions swirling within him cease as his attention is taken by the bare skin of his Mate. A flooding of emotions tingle over his skin. The rise of a distant desire that had become a shadow floats to the surface, whilst battling with those of pure wrath.

Down her back, heavy scars of years taking lashings from her guards are stark against her skin. There's a bright coloring of her skin torn through by darker raised scars from poor healing of her wounds. Lash after lash crossing over her shoulders down to her tailbone, varying of deeper shades of rouge and those of lighter pink from hot blades running over where her wings should appear from.

She has not dared to try making them appear, fearful of the damage they have taken or if they even could form through the heavy scarring that mars her skin.

Alanzo's body becomes still as he watches her carefully step into the tub of warm water, sinking into the bath with a sigh. Not wanting to further give her discomfort after the insidious looks from the incubus below, he shields his emotions of fury for what she will have to live with for the rest of her life.

He steps forward bending low to pick up the clothing from the floor, laying it out on the bed. She leans her head back, watching him as he meticulously sets it all aside. Once he finishes, he pulls his tunic off to reveal his bare chest.

Carmen's gaze softens as she witnesses his own scars. Those from blades across his torso, wounds he sustained from battles he fought to find her. They are few in comparison of what was upon her back, but some are deep along with patches of skin that have suffered burns. All of them holding stories of his search across the world for her. A sinking feeling overcomes her, making her stomach clench as she pushes herself further under the warm water.

Keeping his trousers on, Alanzo comes over with a washcloth and bit of soap that has been set out for them. He drags one of the chairs over, setting it beside the basin Carmen soaks within. She sits further up, water trickling down her shoulders as she moves for him to begin washing her shoulders and back. The cloth is rough over her body, yet he is gentle with every tender movement. Her head tilts to the side as he brushes it over her neck, easing a bit of the tension within her from the unwelcome stares below.

"Do not be ashamed, my heart," he whispers, threading his fingers into her hair to wash it next. She easily tilts her head back as he cups water to rinse the strands.

"I am not," she murmurs. "I am...I feel displaced, Alanzo. Anywhere I may go, there will be no welcome as I dreamt of while in those caverns and battered tents." His movements falter a moment before returning to their task. "My life spent before was for my family...our village and community. Now, I do not know where I belong."

"With me. You belong with me, my life," Alanzo reassures.

Carmen reaches up, water sloshing back into the basin as she grips the hand upon her shoulder. Her fingers clench around his, squeezing in understanding.

"For you are perfection," he continues.

Her head turns a little, cobalt eyes catching his as he gives a gentle look. With his free hand, Alanzo reaches forward and touches her chin with adoration. A smile pulls at her lips, not fully forming as tears threaten to come.

He would be enough. She knew that deep within her core and heart, yet that yearning for a family lingered. It would not leave her. A dream she hoped would come true. Perhaps one day.

"So are you," she says.

Quietly, Alanzo finishes bathing Carmen and she steps out of the basin. He swiftly washes himself with just the washcloth as she begins to eat dinner and he joins her once he finishes. The food is not overtly delicious, but it will do. It was far better than the dry meat and bread that had survived a drowned cave and their long travels.

As they laid down in the bed, softer than any ground they have been sleeping on throughout their long journey, Carmen falls asleep in Alanzo's hold. Within her slumber, she grips him tight as he watches her as the rain continues to fall outside. The lamp off, the dark room surrounds them as the quiet noise of below drifts up through the floorboards.

After some time, Alanzo finally lays down completely and forces himself to rest.

Chapter Ten

"Gratitude is not only the greatest of virtues, but the parent of all others."
– Marcus Tullius Cicero

The rain stopped early morning, bringing bright rays of light through the window. Alanzo brought their morning meal up to their room, not wanting another incident like last night. There were few down in the tavern of the inn, mainly just humans, but he still thought best to bring the meal up. Within a couple of hours, after eating their meal slowly, they left the inn as the sun shone upon the land.

Puddles lined the pathways of the town, now bustling with people as shops opened along the lanes with the smaller trading posts. Alanzo and Carmen pause outside the inn, glancing down the path where the inn keeper said the main market would be. Carmen pulls up her hood, allowing her cloak to keep her head concealed.

They walk out into the thrall of beings, most of them being human. Alanzo does note the large number of werewolves and gargoyles strolling about, even with it being daylight. They stay mainly within the shadows of the buildings, momentarily stepping into the direct sunlight before quickly disappearing into the shade of awnings and looming houses. Carmen's arm repeatedly brushes against Alanzo's, holding her cloak close to her as her eyes dart from being to being. Her rapid heart rate could be felt to her Mate, noting the rising fear inside her from the crowds they navigate.

Near the end of the lane, he directs them down a small path into a shaded area between two tall houses. A small well is down the way of the cobblestone path, a couple of humans using it to wash their linen and clothes.

Silently, Alanzo turns toward Carmen, making her stop in her footsteps before she can begin asking questions. Her wide blue eyes meet his as he eases her back to the towering building, the chilled stone pressing against her back. His hand comes up to caress her cheek, cupping it within the palm of his hand. His other carefully grabs her waist, holding her before him.

"You are safe," he says low, words meant only for her. "No one will take you from me. Never again, my love."

She reaches up, placing her hand upon his as she releases an uneven exhale. Fears simmer below her skin, threatening to drag her under the sea of terrors as flashes of the past come across her mind. The smell of the rain that occurred overnight, warring with her senses as it reminds her of *that* night. The night she was dragged from her house along with others. The fires and the screams. Darkness had surrounded her as they put bags over their heads, and the rough rope around their limbs that cut into their skin. The scent of fresh blood spilling as everything she knew vanished like it had been a dream. Her entire childhood had been a mirage before having to wake to the horrors of that night.

Worst of all he was gone. Alanzo was gone. Everything was gone.

"My heart." Alanzo's voice pulls her back to the present as she squeezes his hand against her cheek. A harsh swallow goes down her throat, barely nodding her head in reply. His head tilts ever so slightly, gaze searching her expression in concern. "We can leave now, if you wish."

"We need supplies. Food," she whispers. "Do not let me endanger our travels."

"You are not endangering us. I could hunt." She shakes her head. "We will survive."

She shakes her head again, shutting her eyes.

Alanzo's thumb caresses over her cheek, gently stroking over her skin as he thinks what to do. He could not ease her worries and fears. If he was the incubus he used to be, then he could use his powers to calm her. He could help keep her in a peaceful manner, free her of the terrible memories that haunted her until they left the town. Except, he could not.

He was not that incubus anymore.

Another thought comes of having her stay outside the town away from the crowd to allow him to buy what they need and then return to her. Except, the very idea of separating from her, even for a short time and a short distance, begins to make his blood writhe. Territorial desires thrash inside him, not willing to let her go out of his sight no matter how 'safe' he could deem this place to be. For his own fears run rampant throughout the trenches of his mind. His own nightmares haunting his steps and thoughts. The last time he left her, she was taken. Never again. Never would he give fate another chance as such.

Alanzo closes his eyes, inhaling a deep breath as he ponders for a solution. It should be simple, and yet such an errand was wrecking both of them. Traveling through forests and even fighting those ghouls was far easier a task than bartering for food from strangers.

Neither of them could rely on their powers to heal the invisible scars. Soothe the other. A reality they have slowly come to realize the past year as they attempted to live near their village again. Many nights and days, both felt they failed the other with the inability to help their Mate. Powerless.

Yet, instinct moves Alanzo forward. He steps carefully closer, engulfing his Mate's body with his as he blocks out the last of the light streaming between the buildings upon her face. His eyes open as she looks up at him. He strokes her cheek again. A warmth flourishes inside him as his other hand slides up her torso, moving towards her back. He presses himself against her, bringing their bodies together as the noise of the town vanishes from his ears.

"Feel me, my life," he speaks low, caressing her under his fingertips. "I am real. I am here."

Her free hand moves, reaching around his waist to feel the warm hardness of his body. Her breathing slows, staring up into those violet eyes. They do not falter from hers as she gently nods her head once. An invitation of tenderness. A quiet yearning to be reminded they are here and not trapped in those nightmares any longer.

Slowly, almost as such when they sat beside that crackling fire, Alanzo leans his head closer. A faint brush of lips of his against hers. Her eyes close, breathing in the delicate scent of Alanzo. Cinnamon. Then comes the mingling of fresh tobacco. Warm and inviting. Another brush of their lips, and then he carefully presses his against hers. Tender is the caress as they hold each other and share a gentle kiss. It alights Alanzo, sparking a deep relief down in his soul that calms him. It wipes away the anger and fears. The small moment washing over him like fresh water from a waterfall; crisp and plentiful.

For Carmen it is a balm to her inner wounds. The screams vanish. The scent of blood and ash drift away, replaced by the faint aroma of Alanzo's natural smell. The simple taste of his lips that are barely even touching hers. It is a delicate and light touch, yet it is a powerful statement of possession.

He pulls back, breaking the connection of their mouths as they flutter their eyes open. His thumb caresses over her cheek again, and a faint smile almost pulls up his lips. Her eyes soften, grasping his fingers as she breathes far easier than she had all morning.

"My knight," she murmurs, and then inhales another long breath before giving him a small nod.

"Keep your hand in mine." The one upon her cheek falls away as he steps back, but their fingers remain intertwined. Her chest squeezes with anxiety, glancing out towards the crowds. She steels herself, straightening as she steps close to Alanzo as he leads them back out into the daylight and crowd.

They remain close, weaving through the crowds until they get to the main market and Alanzo begins quick work of finding food. Carmen keeps her hood up, concealing her head and face as he speaks with a couple of vendors for dried meat, fruit, and bread.

The cadence of his tone helps her remain grounded in the present as she listens to it. Whilst another part of her, thinks of that simple kiss. Their second in years.

Absentmindedly, she lifts her fingers to touch her mouth where his was. Her heart flutters as she follows him, remaining by his side as she recalls the tender touch of his lips. The hand upon her mouth falls as Alanzo buys a few loafs of bread for travel when she overhears a conversation.

"The pass is impossible to venture through, take the route around the mountain," a man speaks, discussing with a vendor next to where they are.

"I shall. I have heard far too many stories of people becoming lost. No one dares to go near that pass," the vendor replies. "I do not have a wish for death or loss of my entire business."

"A few hunters were able to pass through," another mentions.

"Upon almost losing their life and limbs," the first man says. Carmen feels Alanzo's body become tense, sensing him listening into the conversation as well. "The Paranormals won't venture through there either. The winds too strong. Storms violent much like those along the coast."

Alanzo steps back as curiosity flickers within his mind. He leads them over to the next stall where the men talk, glancing over the wares of the vendor that is speaking with them.

"Well, I am only here today, because I must travel tomorrow morning for the next town. And it's a two-week journey to move around that mountain."

"Which mountain do you speak of?" Alanzo asks, barely raising his gaze from the vendor's items.

"To the northwest there are a couple of mountains off the ranges," the vendor explains easily, moving about some of his items of metals. "They are dangerous to cross near. Are you traveling through, incubus?"

"We are."

"Best you avoid it. The few who come through here, even daemons, don't dare to go near that pass. Prepare for longer travel, especially with these spring rains."

"I shall take that into consideration. Thank you." Alanzo nods and has them walk off from the vendor. He does not say anything more as Carmen follows him as he buys a bag of salt, and few other items they hadn't carried before.

"Alanzo?" Carmen's voice drifts as they come to the final stall, and he begins to pack their bag more effectively for travel. "What are you thinking, my knight?"

He glances over at her with a gleam in his eye. "That I may have found our home, my love."

Chapter Eleven

"Do not be afraid; our fate cannot be taken from us... it is a gift."
– Dante Alighieri

The wind would not give any reprieve. It tore at Alanzo's wings as they traveled through the mountain ranges; tunnels of air burst through them like the waves of an angry sea. He had been through many regions across the world of harsh weather, but this was close to becoming the hardest to navigate. Alanzo had become familiar to being on his own, but carrying another through such storms and dangerous gales was becoming a true test of strength.

His back ached from where his wings sprung out from him. They're yanked in different directions he does not wish to go, pushing himself forward as he flies through darkening clouds.

Rain is on the horizon. He could see it. The clouds deepening with a deep grey, while others in the distance are slowly being pulled downward from the heavy water pouring from the heavens.

They had been traveling and searching for hours. There had to be somewhere within this dangerous pass for their home. A place away from civilization and others who would not dare to come find them in such horrible elements. He just needed to survive this. He needed to make it while his Mate is in his arms.

His territorial need for protection and safety pulses through his veins as he pushes forward. Carmen clings to him. They come around another side of a mountain, her fingers grasp him upon approach of the massive storms that brew.

"Alanzo!" Her voice yells over the roaring of the winds that pick up.

He teeters within the sky, tilting downward. A jolt occurs in his body as he tries to descend closer to the trees and forest below them. His gaze hunting through the clouds and haze, searching for anywhere they could land.

Nothing. No clearings. No openings.

The dense forest covers the edges of the mountains, barring him from finding safe areas to land.

His muscles tense. Determination floods him as he glances back at the storms that gather behind them. Lightning abruptly flashes in the skies, illuminating the dark clouds as the last rays of daylight are consumed while the thunder rumbles.

Mind grasping for what to do, he glimpses down at Carmen in his arms. Her head ducks against his shoulder, limbs wrapped around his in a tight hold. Against the cold of the strong winds and incoming storms, he feels her shiver. Alanzo's possessive need roars inside him again, demanding to keep her safe as memories of despair and isolation slam into him.

If anything happens to her...

He shoves away the thoughts, which threaten to drown him before the rains could ever reach them.

Their bodies falter in the skies, dropping as the winds continue their wailing. It whistles through the trees of the forests as Alanzo flies closer. A tenacity of refusal to give in pushes him forward.

As the oncoming darkness of the treacherous thunderstorm looms, he sees a patch between the trees. He aims for the small opening, wings fighting hard against the strong tempests. They reach it, but not before a harsh gale blows causing his wings to be flung backward. They scrape against the branches of the trees, snapping off twigs. The forest rips into Alanzo's wings as he attempts to land as the rain starts to pelt their bodies. Pain blossoms through his back and shoulders, spreading over him as it merges with a stinging sensation.

Carmen yelps as Alanzo barely lands upon his feet. He stumbles, keeping her in his hold as he folds his wings in close to him. He can feel the blood beginning to seep from them; a pulse over his skin. The once long-forgotten pain he had grown familiar to returns with a vengeance to be remembered, causing his steps to falter.

The wind suddenly picks up, rain coming down harder as Alanzo looks to the skies. His jaw becomes rigid, scowling at the horrific weather that blows through the mountains. The men were not wrong in describing the storms throughout this pass, far closer to the ones he had survived while traveling the seas. The winds themselves could produce waves taller than a ship's sails.

Quickly, Alanzo searches around them as the rain stings his sensitive skin. He does not let Carmen go, refusing to let her out of his arms as he moves closer to one of the larger trees with wide branches.

The storm is worsening and there is no other shelter. No cave. No inn. Nothing.

It is them against the elements.

Carmen flinches in his arms, ducking her head as the rain blows through the tree's branches.

Alanzo growls under his breath, anger simmering in his gut at their predicament. Not wasting another moment of her potentially being harmed by the storm, he lets her down. Quickly, he pulls the pack off and she takes it to pull onto her shoulders. He moves for her back to be against the trunk of the tree, engulfing her body with his.

"Alanzo." Her pleading voice pierces deep into his being.

Through the warring of the thunderstorm surrounding them, he could smell it upon her. Within her voice. Her trembling.

Fear. Terror. Dismay.

He steps closer spreading his wings, using them as a shield around them. They ache and hurt. They take the brunt of the raging storm. Alanzo's fingers clutch the tree's bark, keeping his body over hers as he ignores the pain lacing down his back.

He protects her from the worst of the storm, using his body as a wall. His muscles become rigid, tensing against the onslaught that could continue all night or into the next day.

Keep her safe. Keep her safe.

Those words continue to repeat in his mind. They're followed by the memories of loneliness and guilt of not finding her sooner. Long nights searching. Long days tearing apart towns and ships. Years of anguish looking for his love, his life. Torment of the past keeping his focus to protect her.

He would not fail now. He would not lose what he had fought for. And he would find the home that would keep them protected and safe.

His eyes clench shut, keeping his breathing level as he inhales her scent.

Carmen places her hands upon his chest, smoothing them upward.

Ache fills her, witnessing the anguish upon his face he attempts to hide. She does not need to see the lines upon his expression to know the pain he is in. To know the suffering that wrecks her Mate as he shields her from the storm.

Thunder echoes, shaking the trees and ground. She continues to smooth her hands over his chest, hoping to ease any part of him she can. There would be no convincing him to fold his wings in to protect them. Although he was not the same incubus of long ago, she knew enough of this one, the newly molded Alanzo had a stubbornness that could not be destroyed.

He would shield her. Safeguard her from winds, rains, trees, men, ghouls...whatever stood in their path, he would face. He would sacrifice his body, soul, and mind for her.

It was why he found her.

Instead of fighting him as the storm does, she eases her trembling hands over him. Her fingers caress over the base of his throat, smoothing them along the rigid muscles and pulsing veins. His eyes snap open; violet gems glowing in the darkness as he focuses on her. She does not stop, continuing to touch his damp body that is pressed so closely to hers.

Minutes slide into hours. The storm continues, relentless as if designed by Zeus himself. Thunder shakes the earth after every bolt of lightning splits the skies above. Branches snap off and break, tumbling to the forest floor. Leaves are ripped away, blowing through the wind as the other animals of the forest hide.

Alanzo does not move. He does not falter.

His body quakes from exhaustion and hunger.

Keep her safe.

Carmen leans her forehead against his chest. Her head hidden underneath his chin as she presses her body closer against his. He leans more against the tree as her hands remain upon his torso, not quite helping him stand, and yet...she was. Carmen becomes his anchor— the chain tethering him to the earth as the heavens roar above.

They remain under the tree.

The night wears on. The rain beginning to lessen, but then would return with a vengeance. The winds blow through them, making both shiver from the chill. Cold seeps into their bones as they hold fast in the storm.

Hours creep by. Night not moving quickly enough.

Until, finally, daybreak could be seen. Felt.

The harsh gales begin to die down with the storm finally moving on. Trees no long creaking as their branches slide against the other or bowing from the wind.

Stillness comes.

Birds begin to sing. The aftershock of the storm passing as light filters down past the mountainsides and the tips of the trees.

Legs stiff and aching, Alanzo steps back from Carmen as he looks out behind them. His wings droop to his sides as Carmen follows his gaze towards the clearing skies. Without a word, he takes her hand to lead her back to where they had landed.

His hand trembles.

The words in his head to keep her safe do not relent; over and over they sound as his soul becomes weary once more. Rest. But he cannot. Not yet.

"Alanzo?" Carmen's voice rasps. "What are—"

"Leaving."

She gasps, tugging back on his hand as he begins to bring her into his embrace. His tired and damaged wings spread out behind him as he glimpses a moment up into the small opening of trees. New wounds will come when they fly off.

"You are exhausted. Hurt, you cannot fly—"

"I can fly."

"Alanzo, please—"

"Those storms will return." He suddenly grasps her face. Exhaustion lines his features, but his gaze is firm. Determined. Although he is tired and hungry, cold and wet, it will not stop him.

Their chance of finding better shelter was now. Another night could not be lasted here if more storms were on the horizon or if the raging tempests returned. There would be no rest, and then he would have no strength to continue. It had to be now, in hopes of finding a stronger and safer shelter.

"The wind is low. It is warming from the sun. We need to leave now."

Carmen's face is rife with concern, flicking her eyes to the brightening skies. She swallows hard and nods her head.

Alanzo takes her into his arms, having her wrap her limbs around his torso. He clutches the back of her head a moment, inhaling her faint scent. It bolsters his determination, telling himself they're almost there. He can feel it. They've come this far, and he cannot falter.

Yanking his head back, his wings unfurl themselves once more. They scream at him as he pushes them down, bursting up into the trees. Branches scratch at his skin, tugging as they move up into the skies. After bursting through the trees, he flies higher and higher. He adjusts, moving with the light breeze left behind from the night's storms. Carmen clings to him, feeling his body tremble against hers as exhaustion threatens to take him back down to the earth.

He searches. The length of the sun's rays become longer as the early morning stretches on as he flies. It's nearing early afternoon when Carmen feels him teeter. His wings faltering a moment in the skies as they drop a few feet in the air.

"You need rest," she says over the breeze.

"Carmen—"

"You are waning. Rest, my knight. The skies have remained clear." He holds tightly, resolve strong upon his features. "We can rest a few days, and then continue searching."

Hating she is correct; he looks to the right. He glides soundlessly once he sees the tips of shorter peaks. He continues flying over them, looking for a far better option to land where it will not tear his wings apart more. Alanzo can feel the dried blood upon his skin, sticking to him as he sees a clearing.

His body tilts towards it, until he sees a small divide within the mountains of the dangerous pass. Longing hits him as his eyes refuse to leave it, a voice deep within him that calls. Suddenly, he swerves in the air towards the area. Carmen's breathing hitches from the abrupt change as he veers for the split.

This way, the winds are back to being against him. They push at his wings, arms, and entire body which aches for relief. Each down pull of his wings, exhaustion threatens to have him fall from the sky to the ground far below them. He does not stop.

He launches himself faster as Carmen grips him tighter.

"Alanzo!"

"Trust me, my heart!"

He dives between the split of mountain faces, met with a gale that is cold and brutal. Alanzo wanes a moment, fighting back as he soars down through the wide crevice, barely pulling up over a sea of trees. Until, finally, through the low clouds that they spear through, his destination hidden behind the mountain peaks come into view.

A valley. Two small rolling hills within the middle of it, where a wide stream of water flows near the bottom. Tucked away within the chaos of the mountain pass and the large dense swaths of forest is a small, secluded valley.

Alanzo's chest squeezes as he flies down, hearing the gasp out of Carmen's mouth. Body stiffening, he is barely able to land softly upon the first hill. His feet almost tangle over the other as he stumbles across the grass. He stops, wings falling down against his back as his arms loosen around Carmen. She quickly releases him, stepping down upon the damp grass and wildflowers that are drying from the sun.

His heart pounds in his chest, practically feeling Carmen's do the same as they look out at the valley. His tired gaze moves up toward the mountains that surround them, hiding this place from the rest of the world. A forest lines the edges, and perhaps the only path one could venture here on foot, if one was lucky to find it.

Even they must have flown past this place several times before finding it.

The tips of his wings scrape over the grass as all the tension held within his muscles releases. The ache and exhaustion, finally winning as he collapses to his knees. Alanzo lands hard upon the hillside, tips of his fingers reaching into the rich earth. Eyes shutting, relief washes over him.

For the first time in years...he cries.

Alanzo sobs into the hillside with his tears landing upon the wildflowers beneath him.

The last time his tears drenched the earth was for his love being stolen from him; this time it is for finding a safe haven for her. Finally.

Carmen kneels beside him, cradling his head against her chest. He cries as the warm breeze comes, sunlight warming everything around them.

"You found it, my knight... you found it," Carmen whispers, stroking his hair back.

"We—"

"No," she speaks, kissing his head as he begins to clutch at his Mate's clothing. "It was all you, my love...always you. My Alanzo." She chokes out his name, and a deeper sob releases from him.

She holds him close, feeling the weight of the years upon his shoulders lift. A moment, she attempts to reach inside herself for her powers to help ease him but does not find that inkling. Instead, she continues to stroke his back and head as he cries against her skin.

"We're home," she whispers. "Rest, my love. My life...my knight. Finally...rest."

Alanzo cries, body slumping over the grass as trickles of blood drip from his wings. Carmen keeps his head within her lap, smoothing her hand over him as she gently looks to his wounds. Bright sunlight cascades over them.

Tears fill her own eyes as she looks out at the beautiful valley, almost overwhelmed by the prospect of having peace. Somewhere to not be ripped from. Theirs.

She smiles and whispers, "Home."

Chapter Twelve

TEN YEARS LATER

"Fortune sides with him who dares."
- Virgil

Dawn is passing when Carmen closes the gate of her garden. Her hand lingers over the fencing Alanzo built when the animals would not leave her crops alone. Dried grapevines and rope, bought from the village he gets their supplies from, crisscross along the bottom to keep them out.

Basket of vegetables on her hip, she carries it towards the cottage as a couple of their goats come racing around the corner of the small home. They venture out into their grazing area, waking up as the rest of the world around them do.

A few years after they found their home, Alanzo found a village that was closer than the town they visited before finding this valley. It's tucked away as well, a little ways north of the larger mountains that hides them from the world. Every few months, he'll fly to barter with the pelts, minerals, and small items they collect for salt, seeds, metals, or even animals such as the goats, to bring home. Traveling out of the valley has come with trial and error, finding small bouts of time during the year to leave and not be in danger from the weather that surrounds the valley and mountain passes.

She has not stepped foot outside this valley since Alanzo landed upon their hill.

Those were the only lonely days here, when Alanzo was gone for his week-long journeys. In the beginning, it was hard for them. A new nightmare of separation, but with every return and neither of them gone, it became easier with time.

Carmen sets the basket down at the entrance of the cottage, pushing back her long black hair that cascades over her shoulders. Her hands pat down over her skirt and apron, looking out towards where Alanzo is. A smile pulls at her lips as she pulls her hair up into a bun, and then begins to stride down the grassy hill. At the bottom, Alanzo washes their clothes and blankets in the stream that weaves around the hill and disappears into the forest.

Quietly, she begins to sneak up on him as he lays the cloth over their drying rocks for the sun to warm and dry them as it ascends into the sky. He hums loudly to himself, singing one of his favorite lullabies as he works with his back turned towards her.

A moment she takes, pausing in her steps to inhale a long breath of his natural perfume—cinnamon and tobacco. Warm and inviting, a marvelous balm to the soul that balances her sweet blossom scent that surrounds her constantly these days.

A year has passed of both having their powers back, their ability to fully tap into desire, joy, and calm. Pieces of themselves have slowly been sewn back together through patience and love. The peace of their home provided a haven to heal. A place to be vulnerable again. To desire and explore with ideations of hope, not despair.

They did not know much the full extent of what has occurred in the world they've been hiding from for a decade. Alanzo would pick up letters from Giuseppe when he visited the village, along with letters from another shifter he met during his travels. Both were the only beings who knew where the Kraken of the Red Sea resided, hidden from the prosecutions of his deeds.

From the letters, it seemed the world had moved on. Or tried to. It slowly was forgetting the 'monster' who once tormented the seas and oceans of many empires and kingdoms. Rumors were spreading that he had died. Others stating that he had been captured, and now rotted in a cell somewhere in the far north or west.

Her smile softens as she watches him wash their blankets, noticing the joyful grin upon his face.

Ten years. Twice the length of time of them being separated. Their dream had become a reality. After so much pain suffered, some days it still felt like a dream.

Alanzo stands, holding the blanket up before draping it over the rock. His back is completely turned to her, and when nothing is in his hands, she takes her chance. Carmen sprints forward, arms out to tackle him into the stream.

As always, her Mate senses her presence long before she could ever sneak up on him. He spins at the last moment, catching her before she can shove him into the stream. Alanzo's arms go around her, stumbling back into the water as both of them fall in. Water splashes around them as they're drenched in the chilled spring water, rippling over their bodies. Carmen's hair falls out of its containment, loose around her shoulders once more. They sputter a bit, shaking off the water droplets upon their faces.

Alanzo's scent strengthens, happiness flooding out of him as his powers reach out like welcoming arms. His violet eyes glow, coming upon his Mate who grins up at him in his lap. Water swirls around their hips and legs from the soft current of the brook.

"Are you giving me more chores to complete, my love?"

"Never," she muses.

"Yet, here we are wet and cold in the stream." He brings his arm up, water dripping.

"I am not cold, my knight." Her favorite title for him is a whisper of adoration, moving her face closer to his. She cups his face, bringing their lips together for an affectionate kiss. He hums against her. Their powers combine in a flourish that spreads out around them, earnest and blissful.

He kisses her deeper, chest releasing a sigh of contentment.

Alanzo pulls away suddenly, easily standing with her in his arms. Her body wraps around his as water sloshes down from their bodies and drips from their clothes.

"I will still need to get you dry." He walks out of the stream, keeping her in his hold as he starts to venture up the hill towards the cottage he built for her.

"Not going to finish the laundry?" She teases.

"I have the rest of daylight." He smiles broadly.

He stops mid-way up the hill, and his face becomes devious. His scent wraps around her, his powers soothing and brushing over her skin like the softest rabbit's pelt. Alanzo abruptly drops to his knees, laying her down upon the grass of the hill as his body covers hers. His hand strokes down her cheek, kissing her again as the warm spring breeze rustles the grass. The heat of the sun's rays keep them from shivering.

He lays over her, pressing himself to his Mate as he takes his time kissing her. She hums against him, vibrating with desire and happiness.

Alanzo pulls away, looking down at her as the daylight brightens her face. He moves a little to the side, providing more of the sun to shine down upon her as it causes her eyes to sparkle. Gently, he reaches up and moves some of the wet strands of her hair away from her face.

Neither are cold as the sun rises, bringing them a new day.

"Ahh, my beautiful heart," he murmurs.

Her hand comes upon his jaw, thumb caressing over his cheek. "My knight."

He smiles, falling over to his side to lay down next to her in the grass. They remain there in silence as the brilliant dawn breaks over the mountainside completely. Their fingers become intertwined, tightening around the other as Carmen lays her head upon his shoulder. He turns his face into her wet hair, kissing it softly.

After so many years of being lost, they'd found and built their home that was perfect for them. They were happy and would be for many years to come in the valley they had searched so hard for.

At long last, the incubus and his heart had found their home.

For now.

Want to know what happens to Alanzo & Carmen in 600 years?

You can read all about them and the family they finally have in the first book of the "Mafia, Murder, and Mayhem Series":

"Vinny the Vampire & Me"

Or

You can read about them in the short story anthology about them adopting their youngest child in the prequel to the main series:

"Memories of the Underground: Volume One"

Books by Elm Jed

Mafia, Murder, and Mayhem Series
Paranormal Mafia

Vinny the Vampire & Me
Sweet Cheeks & Her Mob Boss
The Wolf Boss & His Darling
The Werecat & Her Lone Wolf: A Novella
The Goth & The Housewife: A Novelette
Memories of the Underground: Volume One

Contemporary BDSM Series
My Dear Watson
My Forgotten Demons
My Emerald Fire
My Dear Leo

About the Author

Elm Jed is an award winning author, who mostly writes mafia, paranormal, and suspense romance. They are a disabled, queer, Marine Corps veteran, who's been writing since they were ten years old with a degree in Theatre. Their books focus on mental health awareness and giving readers a space to feel seen in different ways from disabilities to understanding their queerness.

You can keep up with what Elm Jed is doing by signing up to their newsletter on their website: https://elmjedauthor.com/

www.ingramcontent.com/pod-product-compliance
Lightning Source LLC
LaVergne TN
LVHW050935080826
845145LV00004B/1267

* 9 7 8 1 9 6 7 0 1 9 2 1 2 *